Grave Markers
Volume 1

Richard Black, Sebastian Bendix,

and Joshua Rex

A
Grinning Skull Press
Publication

ISBN: 0-9973882-0-X
ISBN-13: 978-0-9973882-0-6

CONTENTS

A WORD ABOUT GRAVE MARKERS

I promise to keep this short so you can get on to reading the tales collected in this volume. Folks often ask about Grave Markers and what they are. Grave Markers are, in a word, novelettes. They are stories too long to be included in anthologies (which usually average 5,000 to 7,000 words) but not quite long enough to be published on their own as stand-alone novellas. They are published individually in digital formats, and then later compiled into a print collection. The reason why we started this line is we often heard authors commenting that there wasn't a market for those "in-between" length stories and we wanted to give them an outlet for such pieces. And that about sums it up. Told you I'd keep it short. Now, without further ado, I present to you the premier collection of Grave Markers. Enjoy!

Michael J. Evans
Grinning Skull Press

i

GRAVE MARKER

Richard Black

Nikolis Cole
THE LOW-RISE SAINT

CHAPTER ONE

Detective Karen Oswalt kicked her feet up on her desk, folding a newspaper open to the Sudoku page. Her partner, Leon Barnes, was sitting in the same cubicle, flicking through a gaming magazine.

"Shit," Leon said, "the new 'Car Jacker' looks tight."

Karen looked up at him, pencil dangling from between her lips.

"I can feel your judgemental gaze on the top of my head," Leon said. He sat back and folded his arms. "What?"

Karen took the pencil out of her mouth, thought for a moment, then smiled. "'When I was a child, I spoke as a child, I understood as a child, I thought as a child, but when I became a man, I put away childish things'."

Leon stared at her blankly for a moment. "Fuck you say to me?"

"You're forty-five years old, Leon."

"First of all," he said, brandishing the magazine, "you know I hate it when you get that Holy Virgin smile on your face and quote shit from the Bible. Creeps me the fuck out. Second of all, forty-five

3

is the new fifteen. Third of all, nothing childish about 'Car Jacker', it's rated M, for Man."

"Pretty sure the M's for Mature."

"Then I'm fucking mature. Same difference."

Karen laughed. "I'm not a man," she said, "and I'm mature."

"Well, you know what I mean."

"It's a game."

"A mature game, for men."

"Games are for children, Big Man."

Leon wheeled his chair over to Karen and grabbed the newspaper from her lap. "What do you call this?"

She snatched it back. "This," she said, rolling up the paper and smacking him on the head with it, "is a puzzle, that challenges the brain and helps to enhance its ability to process various forms of information, details, images, and strategies. It makes me a better cop. What does 'Car Jacker' teach you? That kicking a woman to death regenerates your health?"

Leon shrugged. "No," he said, rubbing his head, "only kicking prostitutes to death. You roll a lead pipe up in that thing? Damn. Anyway, the game teaches you lots of other things."

"Like what?"

"It improves hand–eye coordination, reflexes. Teaches you about criminal psychology—"

"Bullshit."

"I'm telling you, Karen, you can learn a lot from video games. Just a matter of time before they start using them as teaching tools at the Academy."

"Yeah," she said, marking a couple of numbers in the Sudoku grid. "Same Academy where Steve Guttenberg got his badge? Forgive me if I don't take advice on how to be good poh-lice from a guy who's just back from a six-month suspension."

"Jesus, Oswalt," Leon said. He leaned back, folded his arms across his chest in a sulk.

Karen threw down her puzzle. "I'm sorry, Leon, I was just bustin' your balls."

He looked at her, frowned, and said "It was a justified kill, Karen. The suspension was bullshit."

Karen scratched her nose, cleared her throat, then said, "I know." She gave him a reassuring smile. "I know, Leon."

"Um, sorry to interrupt."

They looked up to see the new guy, a skinny kid named Daniels, standing over them.

Leon cleared his throat. "What's up, Toothpick?" he asked, playing with his tie.

"I, uh ..." He pointed his thumb over his shoulder. "I got a Slug here, on the phone."

"Slug," Karen said, smiling. "Motherfucker. Long time since I heard that name."

"Shit," Leon said, awkwardly crab-walking his chair back to his desk. "I was starting to think he was lying dead in an alley somewhere. What the prodigal sonofabitch want?"

"Beats me," said Daniels, scratching the back of his neck. "Says he'll only talk to Karen, and, uh, the fat ginger Mick."

Karen laughed. Leon grunted through his nose and threw down his magazine.

"Put the call through," Leon said. As Daniels turned to go, he added, "And, son. If you ever call me ginger Mick again, I'll cut off your dick and stick it in my freezer, along with all the other pricks of pricks that ever called me a ginger Mick."

Daniels opened his mouth to defend himself, but Karen shot him a glare that said, *Don't you do it if you value your life.*

He shut his mouth and nearly fell over himself as he walked off.

"Bullshit," she said, laughing and shaking her head.

"What?" Leon asked, placing his hand on the phone.

"You got no room in your freezer for cocks, with all those bottles of vodka and frozen pizzas."

Leon rolled his eyes, then picked up the receiver. He held the mouthpiece to his chest and said, "Think I'm gonna go ask Daniels to be my new partner. You and me, this shit right here—" He pointed back and forth between them. "—ain't gonna work out."

Karen smiled, opening a drawer and pulling out a notepad. "Been saying that every damn day for seven years."

"Mean it every damn day I say it, too."

* * *

"Slug, you motherfucker," Leon said into the phone. "Where you been?"

Karen wheeled over on her chair to listen in.

"Sorry, man," the high-pitched voice said. "I been lying low. Street's been crazy.""

"Tell me something I don't know, asshole."

Karen pulled back. "Jesus, Leon," she whispered. "Take it easy."

"Listen here, street trash," he went on, ignoring her. "I have informants like you down on the corners to keep me in the know so I can stop these assholes dropping bodies. There's genocidal shit going on out there and where the fuck have you been?"

"I'm sorry, man, I—"

"It's detective to you, you perma-fried cocksucker. Detective Fat Ginger Mick."

"Sorry, Detective."

Karen grabbed the phone from her partner and placed her hand over the mouthpiece. "Dumbass," she said, glaring. "Twelve months without a solid informer and one finally lands back on our doorstep and you want to scare him off?" She shook her head. "Grow the fuck up."

Leon opened his mouth to protest but said nothing. He flicked his tie, folded his arms, and sat back.

Karen shook her head. "M for Mature my ass." She took her hand off the mouthpiece. "Slug, it's Karen."

"Oh. Hey, girl."

"You got something for us, son? Or you just call to give ol' Leon a coronary?"

Silence.

"It's a kinda delicate situation," he said. "I don't feel cozy talkin' on the phone. Can we meet? Same place as a year ago?"

"Bodies or drugs, Slug?" Karen asked. "I'm homicide now. If it's drugs, I can put you in contact with some good guys over at narcotics."

"Oh, it's definitely bodies, Detective. Usual place, and bring the fat man."

"Slug, hold up—"

The line went dead.

Karen grinned as she put down the phone.

"What the junkie have to say?" Leon asked, watching Karen as she stood up and pulled on her grey suit jacket.

"Come with me, Big Man. I think we just landed ourselves back in the game."

Leon groaned and stood up. "I hate it when my routine is interrupted by some real police work."

CHAPTER TWO

"Where the fuck is that cocksucker?" Leon said, rubbing his huge hand over his belly. "If I knew we'd be waitin' half the damn night, I would have brought a lil' somethin' to sustain a man."

The two cops were sitting in an unmarked car on a street of run-down, red brick row houses. Karen was behind the wheel.

"You expect a junkie to be punctual, Leon?"

Leon said nothing.

Karen sighed, peering out the window at the dark, empty streets.

The block had been surrendered to the gangs long ago. People had abandoned their homes, and then the junkies had moved in. Most of the buildings had no running water and no electricity. It was one of dozens of neighborhoods within the city that had been boarded up and left to crumble. Urban decay didn't just refer to these abandoned blocks, but also the people, their bodies decaying from disease and malnutrition; that is, if they weren't lucky enough to die from a hot shot or an overdose first.

"Look at this," Karen said, pointing a chewed-up finger nail around at their grim surroundings. "Every damn year another block becomes a graveyard for the living." She frowned, shaking her head. "Shit, the only reason they don't knock these places to the ground isn't because the rats would come pouring out of here—it's because the people would. They need wastelands like these so they can bury people here. It's a fucking epidemic swept under the rug."

"Shit, Karen," Leon said, smirking. "If I didn't know any better, I'd say you've caught a severe dose of social concern. You fuck a missionary or somethin'? You can catch it that way, you know."

Karen shrugged. "Ugly, is all."

Leon shook his head. "There's drugs everywhere, Karen. Long time since it was just a ghetto disease."

"Yeah," Karen said, raising an eyebrow, "but when someone gets shot, or dies of a bad dose in the 'burbs, it's not just us two mopes sent to look into it. We get majors, colonels, and deputy commissioners breathing down our necks. We get a special detail and other cases are put on hold. The mayor and Channel 7 are constantly on the line asking to be updated on the situation." She sighed. "Drugs are everywhere, Leon, but the war is being fought out here. This is where we should be making a stand, not waving the white flag."

A knock on the passenger-side window. A jumpy, skeletal-looking white kid stood outside. He sported a denim jacket covered in functionless buttons and a brown baseball cap on his head. Karen stuck her thumb toward the back seat.

The boy opened the door and hopped in. "Dee-tect-iives."

Karen turned in her seat.

"Damn, Slug," Leon said, cringing as he examined the pathetic-looking image in the rear view mirror. "You look like a scarecrow stuffed with dog shit."

Slug squirmed in his seat, scratching underneath his cap. "Good to see you too, man."

Karen glared at her partner, who merely shrugged in response and lit a cigarette. She sighed, turned to Slug, and smiled. "So, Slug, it's been a while. Where you been at?"

He licked his cracked lips and started picking at an ugly looking brown scab on his nose. "Yeah, sorry 'bout that," he said. "Been laying low this past while. It's been warfare down here lately, as y'all know. No need to be a player to catch a bullet these days, pay no mind to killin' a citizen no more. Rules have changed, no longer no code."

Leon laughed. "There was never any code, Slug." Just a bunch of killers callin' themselves soldiers."

"Hey, those guys may have been stone-cold killers, but these guys ..." He shook his head. "They're animals."

"Yeah," Karen said. "It's fucked up. So, you gonna help us catch some of these perpetrating motherfuckers, or what?"

"Yeah," Leon said. "How 'bout you tell us why you dragged our asses all the way out here."

"A-ight," Slug said. "I hear ya. Down to business. You guys remember Lil' Zippo, right?"

Leon and Karen looked at each other. Leon dropped his cigarette on his lap. He cursed and flicked the butt out the window.

"Sure," Karen said. "One of Eddie Holmes' boys."

"Not just another soldier," Leon added, wiping ash from his lap. "His first Lieutenant. Blood, too. His sister's boy."

"That's the guy," Slug said, making a feeble effort to snap his fingers.

"Yeah," Karen said, nodding. "Disappeared six months ago. Eddie reckons Belial Shaitan took him out. It's what started this damn war in the first place."

"Correct, officer. Seems you got another snitch out there 'sides good ol' Slug."

"No," Leon said, "just good, old-fashioned surveillance work. Get to it, boy."

"Just 'bout to. See, Lil' Zippo weren't killed by no Bel Shaitan."

Leon shrugged as he lit another cigarette to replace the one he dropped. "Never thought he was," he said. "Not Bel's style to make a body disappear. Much rather throw it out onto the street all mutilated and shit for the whole neighborhood to see."

"So," Karen said, "you know who iced Zippo, huh?"

"Yeah, yeah," Slug said. "Weren't no hopper, no gangster neither. No, no, was somethin' way more fucked up. Was somethin' freaky, not even real life, know what I'm sayin'?"

"I don't speak junkie," Leon said, exhaling through his nose.

"This ain't no junkie talk, brother. I was on that corner that night, see that Lil' Zippo get fucked up and dragged off the street."

Leon punched the dash so hard the glove box popped open. He

spun around. "You motherfucking dope fiend," he growled, shaking his fist. "You piece of shit dog-kickin' crackhead. You witness a murder? You know who killed Holmes' boy, Zippo, and you didn't come to us?"

Karen put her hand on Leon's shoulder, and he instantly shrugged it away. He was trembling. His face darkened. Sweat beaded on his brow.

"Worst of all," he shouted. "You know it wasn't Shaitan. Holmes thinking it was is what started all this shit in the first place."

"I ... I know man."

"Do you?"

Slug whimpered, sinking back in his seat. "I'm real sorry. I was just scared to come to you after—"

"Shut the fuck up," Leon growled. "You fucking shut your mouth." Leon pointed his finger in Slug's face, breathing like an angry bull. He finally clenched his fist and sat back into his seat, biting once deeply into his knuckles.

Karen stared at Leon, a look of confusion and worry on her face.

Leon took a deep breath, closed his eyes, exhaled. He looked at Karen and smiled. "Sorry, Karen," he said. "I lost it there for a sec." He held up his hands. "My bad."

"God damn right, your bad," she said. "What the fuck, Leon." She turned to Slug. "Sorry about that, Slug, but you gotta understand, it's been a hell of a year. Hell, it's been a Hell Year. The bodies have been piling up and there's been no new leads, no new evidence. We could have really used you back when all this shit started."

Slug sniffled, wiped his nose with the sleeve of his jacket, leaving a silvery trail. "I know, Karen," he said. "I sorry, girl. I lose friends in this shit, too. You know I always give you the goods, always. But what I saw … I didn't think no one would listen, 'specially coming from a dope fiend like me. 'Sides, after that night I try get clean, you know? Been clean a long time."

Karen reached back and touched his hand, squeezed it, smiled. "Hey," she said. "Good for you."

Slug smiled. Leon groaned. Slug frowned.

"On the street again though, 'shamed to say. Good news is, I can get to work for you guys again, anything you need. First, I just need you to hear me out, maybe do Slug a little favor."

"Tell us about the murder," Leon said. "Then we'll talk favors."

"All right," Slug said, "but you, you gotta hear me out 'til the end, all right, you gotta give me that."

"Motherfucker," Leon said, shaking his head and rubbing the bite marks on his knuckles, "I don't gotta give you shit, but since I've been waiting a whole damn year to hear this story, I guess we'll hear you out."

CHAPTER THREE

"I was shakin' out, you know? Cold December, no money, no drugs. Desperation setting in. I had no choice. I left my shit hole and went to the corner, the one Zippo be at. I seen him give other brothers credit before, and I be a good customer so I think I be entitled to some of that.

"Walked up and there three kids working. Zippo was smokin', leanin' on that old rusty ass Mercedes of his. That fat kid Gonzo was sitting on the stoop minding the package. Girl I don't know, a real little one, was pacing back and forth all nervous, like it be her first day."

"I know Gonzo," Leon interrupted, "but this girl, can you describe her?"

Karen took out a notepad and pen.

"Real little, like a circus freak, you know? Hair all in dreads, like a hundred piercings in each ear."

Karen scribbled this down, then rested the pad on her knee.

"So you walked up to the corner boys," Leon said. "What next?"

"Walked up, say yo, try and give him a brotherly handshake and he just stares through me. He say you got no business here then you better step off, white boy. I step back. I look at the others, they starin' at me, too. I think about walkin' way, but shit—the bugs are crawlin' all over so I say, real close and quiet like, I say, 'Listen, brother, I ain't got no coin, not tonight, but I be down this way to-morrow, like you know I be down here every day. I sort you out good, for the product and little something extra for you own self. What you say? You know I a local man, I good for it.'

"So he snorts and spits and smiles and turns to the two others and says, 'Yo, you hear this stupid motherfucker?' Then the two stand up and walk closer and then Zippo say, 'Asshole 'spects me to give him what he needs for free!'

"Gonzo laugh like Santa Claus, belly all wobblin' and jigglin'. The little one say, 'Fo' free? He think we running a fuckin' charity shop up in here?' I remind him I don't want nothin' for free, I pay him back, I a honest man, whatever else they wanna say 'bout me, no one ever had no cause to call me a liar. Then he gets all up in my face and say, 'You nothin' but a dope fiend, and all dope fiends liars. Now step off, motherfucker!'

"I back away, but the girl come up anyway, push me to the ground and shout, 'Step off, bitch!' And I tryin', I tryin' to step off. I tryin' to get up off my ass, then the fat man come up and go kick me in the gut. I yell out. Zippo gets in there and kicks me in the ribs, laughin' like he havin' the time of his life. I get to my feet and that little bitch kick me in the nuts. Fat man punches me in the face and I out. I'm on the road on my back, feel like I sinking under water. I ... I think I pass out."

Karen was getting a bad feeling about this. She'd heard the story a million times before. "So, Slug, you passed out ..."

"Let me guess," Leon said. "You woke up, maybe a weapon in your hand, Zippo dead, you can't remember a thing?"

Slug looked at Karen, then at Leon as they both waited for what they were sure was coming. He burst out laughing. "You guys think I killed him?"

"Did you?" Leon asked. "Your story so far sounds like a killer justifying himself."

"Yo, yo, yo, hold up," Slug said, waving his hand. "I didn't kill Zippo. Jesus Christ, you must really think I'm crazy. I don't have the balls to kill anyone, let alone a gangsta. Officers, if I killed everyone that ever roughed me up you'd have a serial killer on your hands. I'm kinda the neighborhood hacky sack, not a week goes by without some hopper spilling my blood in the gutter."

"All right, Slug," Karen said, holding up her hand. "We hear you."

"Now can I finish my story, unless you don't wanna know who the real killer is."

"Please," Leon said. "Sooner we wrap this shit up, sooner I get me some KFC wrapped in Domino's."

Karen gave Leon a look. *Really?*

"What?" he said, raising an eyebrow. "You never have a Colonel's Calzone before?"

Ignoring them, Slug continued. "I woke up. There be gunshots. Screamin'. I grab the bumper of Zippo's ride and haul my ass up. I don't know where I am for a time, there be blood in my eyes and I scared stupid. Then I remember. Zippo. Motherfucker!

"I wipe my eyes, holding my ribs as I walk cos it hurt. The ground slips away under my feet and I balance myself upside the wall. Takes a second for my eyes t'focus, then I see the bag tucked in under the steps of the porch. The fuckin' supply. I look around, no sign of Zippo's crew. I walk over to the paper bag and open it and it be full of dope. For one stupid second I think about taking the whole bag, but considerin' I ain't got no death wish I take half a dozen vials and stuff 'em in my pocket."

"Wait ..."

"Jesus, Leon, let him finish."

"Just one thing. You said you heard gunshots and screaming."

"That's what I said."

"And you hang around the street in the wide open?"

"Hey man, that night I would have taken a bullet in the head just for one hit. If I didn't take that shit I woulda crawled back in my hole, smashed a bottle of Jack, and cut open a fuckin' vein, or sank into the subway, jumped in front of the midnight train. I had the Dick Tracy's real bad, Leon, real bad."

"All right, all right," Leon said with a wave of his hand. "What next?"

"I feel somethin' pokin' into back my head, and I know I fucked up. I close my eyes 'specting whoever it was to pull the trigger for sure. But they don't. Hear a voice say, 'Git up, white boy, nice and slow.' Open my eyes and stand up, slow just like he said. Then he wrap his arm 'round my neck real tight and pull me in close. He sticks the gun in my ear, his face right by mine."

"Who's face?" Karen asked, clutching the pen. "Details, Slug, please."

"Right, sorry. It be Zippo. And he scared."

"Scared?"

"Real scared. I can feel his cold sweat on my face and the barrel of the pistol rattlin'. He start backing away onto the road shouting, 'See what I got? I got your boy!'"

"What?" Leon asked.

"Hell, I don't know what he talkin' 'bout. I start say somethin' and he stick the gun into my ear real hard. I cry out and he yell, 'Shut up or I put a hole in your fuckin' head, white boy.' Then he look out into the dark, shouting crazy. He yell, 'You hear that! I say I gonna kill your boy. Now show yourself, fool.'"

"This is getting interesting," Leon said.

"We cross the street and he bring me down an alley. 'Spose he didn't want nobody comin' at him from behind. He crouch behind a dumpster and drag me down, pushin' my face into the ground. He hold my head down, but I roll up my eyes, see him point his gun out over the dumpster. He ask me what I do. I say I didn't do nothin'. He ask me if I pay some psycho to cut up his crew. I tell him no and he call me a lyin' motherfucker. Then he say who that?

"He take his hand off me and stick his knee in my neck. I can barely breath. I turn my head 'round as much I can and see him staring out, two hand wrapped 'round the gun. Then his eyes and his mouth open up real wide. He shouting, 'You get back, motherfucker!'

"He shoots off a couple of shots, I cry out, he punch me in the head. He dig his knee in deeper. Now I can't breathe at all. Finally, he get up off me and stand, walks out from behind the dumpster pointin' his gun. Takes me a while to catch my breath, was close to blackin' out again. I put a hand on top of the dumpster and lift myself to my knees. I look over at Zippo. He yellin' somethin' but I can't hear right, like water in my head or somethin'. I try to stand up and I wobble around, fall on my ass. Then I try again, get up, look over the dumpster.

"It was dark, I only see the shadowy shape of a dude against the street light shinin' behind him. Before I can make him out, Zippo grab me by the collar, pull me into his chest and point the gun at my head. He shout out, 'You gonna die for this, fool!' And as he say it, I thinkin', *Dang, who the hell would die for this fool? Who would go up against Shaitan's boys to save my skinny white ass?*

"Zippo lets go of me, pushes me against the wall. He shootin' his gun, screamin' like a crazy motherfucker. I sit on the ground, close my eyes, and cover my ears.

"It goes all quiet, so I open my eyes and I see Zippo's kicks, his fuckin' feet danglin' in the air in front of me. I look up and see some-one got him by the throat, holdin' him up with one hand. Fiend must be strong, too, 'cos you've seen Zippo, he ain't exactly skin and bone.

"I back up against the wall, try and hide myself in the trash. I rip a garbage bag as I'm pulling it over me and spill nasty juicy all over. Man, worst stink I ever smelt in my life. But I'm crappin' my pants, man. All I wanted to be right then was a bag of garbage. I mean, I'm trying to cram my skinny ass *inside* the bag.

"Then I hear a sound and, man, even thinkin' 'bout that sound now makes me wanna bring up my Micky D's. It was like a crunch and a pop, and then I watch Zippo drop in a pile in front of me. He looked like one of those freaky lookin' wooden puppets with the strings cut off.

"I'm lookin' at him and see his fuckin' head is twisted the wrong way round. I mean, *nasty*, right? I try not to scream. I can hear the guy walkin' away. I put my hand over my mouth, hold my breath, then Zippo opens his mouth and *he* screams. Then, course, you know, *I* scream. I mean, what the fuck, right? I didn't think no one could still be breathin' with their head half twisted off like that. It was sick.

"Zippo stopped screamin'. I slapped my hand over my mouth again. I looked at Zippo, thinkin' he might be dead, but he's alive. He's staring at me, blood bubbling from his nose like cookin' Caca. Motherfucker looks like he still tryin' to kill me, like he thinks he can stick me with his eyes. I'm staring back at him, thinkin' the movies are fuckin' bullshit. Ain't nothin' sneaky or ninja or CIA about snappin' a brother's neck, that shit's a hundred percent gangsta."

"Zippo opens his mouth to scream again, but I kick him hard in the teeth. He closes his eyes and groans, breathing so loud through his nose it sounds like he's snoring, fast asleep without a care in the world. I about to kick him again and, you gotta understand officers, it was self-preservation, Zippo was making a racket, man, and it was gonna get me killed."

"But he was breathing," Karen asked.

"Ya, ya, as I was sayin', I was gonna boot him again, hoping he'd stop breathin' 'cos he was breathin' too loud! But just as I raised my foot a boot came down and stomped on his head. And I mean *stomped.* Zippo's jaw was twisted off, his nose was mush, and his eye sockets were just, just gone, crushed like beer cans.

"I looked at the boot as it scraped across the concrete, wiping off Zippo's … I guess Zippo's brains. I close my eyes, thinkin', *This is it, Slug, a shitty end to a shitty life!* I wait and wait, but nothin' happens. I think he must be gone, but when I open my eyes, he's still there. I look up. I was gonna look into his eyes and beg for mercy, only this fiend, he ain't got no eyes."

"The fuck you mean, no eyes?" Karen asked.

"Well, he ain't got no eyes, 'cos motherfucker ain't got no head."

CHAPTER FOUR

"That's it!" Leon kicked open the door,

"Aw hell," Karen sighed, jumping out after him. She stood and leaned on the roof of the car as Leon dragged Slug out onto the pavement. "Leon, take it easy. You'll give yourself a heart attack."

He hauled Slug to his feet and pinned him up against the red brick wall. "You stupid sack of shit," he yelled, spraying Slug's face with saliva. "You telling me some hard-done-by headless junky came back from the dead and killed Zippo and his boys? You think I got nothing better to be doing than wasting my time listening to your fairy tales?"

"I'm not lyin'!" Slug shouted, blubbering, tears dribbling down his cheeks. His legs trembled and gave way so that the only thing holding him up was Leon's fists clutched around his coat. "You know how Bel do business. You fuck with him and you get got, and when you dead, you get got again. You know all those John Does you be findin' all fucked up down by the low rises? All burned up, cut up, sometimes with their heads cut off? Well, this guy was one of those John Does, 'cept he didn't stay dead."

Leon laughed. "And why, pray tell, didn't this beheaded fuck kill you?"

Slug shrugged. "I dunno, man. He just helped me up and gave me a burrito."

"Motherfu ..." Leon held a fist above his head and was about to yell some more when Karen placed her hand on his shoulder.

"Leon," she said. "A word."

He looked at her hand, then met her eyes. He let go of Slug, who fell to the ground in a heap. They walked over to the car. Karen stepped close to his ear.

"Maybe we should hear the rest of this fairy tale," she said.

"You shitting me?" Leon said, pointing toward the pile on the ground. "That boy is bat shit, finally gone and cooked his brains for good."

"Maybe."

"Maybe?" He laughed. "You think we should call up Ichabod Crane to consult with us on this? Hear he's after a guy fitting the same description."

"Funny," Karen said, rolling her eyes. "Listen, Leon, maybe somewhere in all this delusional junky shit is the truth. Let's hear him out. It's not like we got any other leads."

Leon grinned, shook his head, then removed a pack of cigarettes from his pocket. "Aight," he said, "Fucking entertaining if nothing else I 'spose."

He lit a cigarette, walked with Karen over to Slug and helped him to his feet. He dusted off Slug's shoulders and offered him a cigarette.

Slug nodded, smiled slightly, and slid a stick from the pack with a shaky hand. "Thanks, man."

Leon dropped the pack back in his pocket. "I don't want thanks, Slug,' he said. "I want answers."

"I got a name," Slug said with a shrug. "And I know where he hang."

CHAPTER FIVE

"Who the fuck is Nikolis Cole?"

"Oh," Slug said, half chuckling, "he just a junkie like me. But he something of a legend 'round here. We used to call him Saint Nikolis, 'cos he was always quotin' the Bible. Old Testament mostly, real fire-and-brimstone shit. He used to bring a chair out onto the yard on Sundays and preach to the young 'uns. Sure, he was a crackhead, but he was like a grandpa to all the crackheads on the block. He didn't take no shit from no gangsters neither. I told you before, these guys like to mess us around just for fun. We pay their wage, we pay their lively hood, and they treat us like shit at their feet. But Cole ..." Slug laughed. "Heh, if he see any of those hoppers pickin' on any of the boys, he'd get right up in their faces. Lord knows why they didn't give him a beatin'. I'd say maybe they respect their elders but I've seen them give old ladies the same abuse they give everybody else.

"They finally got back at the ol' man though. I guess Bel Shaitan got word that some low-life junkie had been disrespectin' his crew."

"So this Cole killed Zippo and his boys?" Leon asked.

"Yeah," Slug said, "but, you have to understand, it was justified, seein' as they cut off his head n' all."

"Riight."

Slug was walking in front of them. He led them past a boarded-up chop shop. Firelight flickered in the rusted-out holes in the garage door, the sound of clinking bottles and laughter drifted out from inside. They walked into a dilapidated concrete skate park littered with graffiti, trash, shattered beer bottles, and vial glass.

"We should have called for backup," Karen said.

Leon laughed. "Karen, girl, if you want to call in, tell headquarters we're closing in on the infamous headless horseman, you go right ahead."

At the rear of the skate park, Slug pushed aside a hedge and lifted the flap of cut wire fence behind it.

"We just have to tell them we're following a lead," she said, crouching and pushing through the fence. She stood up at the other side and turned around. Slug pulled the wire back further to accommodate Leon's girth.

"Whatever, Karen," he said, grunting and huffing as he grabbed a clump of grass and heaved himself through. "This is your show, fucking freak show that it is." He stood up, brushed off his knees. "It's your call."

"It's not my call; it's *protocol*," she said. "God, my twelve-year-old boy doesn't whine as much as you, and he's a little shit."

Slug had already come through the fence. He pulled the wire

back into place and walked between the two cops without looking at them. "Come on, detectives." He walked quickly through an overgrown square surrounded by low-rise apartments. "Saint Nik's gonna be here soon. He don't ever miss an appointment, know what I'm sayin'?"

Leon ran to catch up. Karen jogged behind. She took out her phone and dialed the precinct. She wasn't calling for backup; she had decided to just check in with their location and update them on the situation.

Leon caught up and grasped Slug's skinny shoulder in his baseball mitt of a hand. Slug's legs nearly ran out from under him as he was jerked backward. "Slow down, asshole," Leon said, out of breath.

Karen snapped her phone shut as she walked up beside them. "Weird."

Leon turned around.

"Tried ringing the station," she said, "and all I heard was static."

"No signal?" Leon asked

"No, I mean, fucking static, like on a radio."

Leon raised an eyebrow. "That ain't the only thing that's weird."

The two cops looked around. The housing project was eerily deserted. The market for narcotics operated at its peak between 5 pm and 4 am. It was 10:35 pm. There should have been half a dozen teenage dealers hanging around yelling "Pandemic" or "China White", and scores of zombie-looking addicts lining up to get their fix, but only the three of them stood in the central square. The only sign that they weren't alone was the lights shining through drawn curtains in a couple of the barred windows.

"What the hell is going on here, Slug," Karen said, unconsciously resting her thumb on the grip of her gun. "Everyone gone on vacation?"

Slug laughed, tugged on his eyebrow hair. "Um, I guess things have been slow 'round here with all the killin' n' all."

"This isn't slow," Leon said, casting a worried look around their surroundings, "this is fucking post-apocalyptic."

"Yeah, I guess it's kind of weird, huh?" Slug said, scratching his neck. His paleness and sweat-beaded brow lay nakedly exposed in the unusually bright moonlight. "So, we should get goin', officers, if you wanna catch this guy."

He turned and put his hand on the railing of a flight of steps.

"Hold it," Leon said.

Slug froze, and after a moment turned around. His Adam's apple rose and fell in a gulp, then he smiled.

Leon looked up the stairs, then left and right along the walkway on the upper floor. There were two illuminated windows, just enough light for him to see that there was no one standing outside. He looked at Karen, who looked just as unsure.

"Fuck this, Leon," she said, stepping back and unsnapping her holster. "I don't like this one bit."

"Damn right," Leon said. He lifted his right arm in Slug's direction and signaled *Come 'ere* with his hand.

Slug looked up the stairs and put his foot on the first step.

"Slug!" Leon yelled.

Slug's body jerked, then he turned slowly, holding up his hands. He was crying.

"What are ya doin'?" Slug asked. He wiped snot away with his sleeve. "You gotta git 'im, man." He looked at Karen. "You guys gotta git 'im."

Leon approached him and grabbed his upper arm. He tugged him away from the steps. "We're going back to the car and we're gonna call for back up. I don't know what this is, Slug, but I have a feeling you're trying to fuck us."

Slug struggled in Leon's grip. "Whatcha gotta call back up for? I ain't tryin' to fuck you, man."

Leon stopped, released his grip and gave him a shove. Slug staggered and would have fallen on his ass if Karen hadn't grabbed him. "You don't want us to call back up, Slug, huh?" Leon tilted his head sideways. "Now why might that be?"

Somewhere between the shove and Karen breaking his fall, Leon had drawn his weapon. He was tapping the barrel against his thigh.

Karen stared at the gun in Leon's hand as she helped Slug to his feet. He trembled in her hands, a combination of DT's and fear.

"Leon, put that thing away," Karen said. "Christ, you're just back from suspension, you really want this kid reporting that you were waving your piece in his face?"

Leon looked at her, mouth hung open for a moment in disbelief. "I'm not waving it in his fucking face. Jesus." He laughed, looked up at the tall buildings that loomed over the low-rise project, then turned his gaze to the moon.

It was shining too brightly for the city. Normally the moon's glow was dulled by the light and fuel pollution, but there it shone. He looked back at Karen and said, "We agreed, Karen, it was a good shooting. Hell, you backed me up at the hearing."

"Put it away," she said, waving his hand down.

Leon looked at her, then at Slug. He looked at his gun before holstering it. "It was a good kill, Karen."

She shrugged. "I trusted you then, I still trust you. We're partners. Now, how 'bout you shut the fuck up about it." She looked at Slug. "Not exactly the time or the place."

Leon peered at Slug. "What you looking at?"

Slug's gaze dropped to the grass. "No—nothin', man."

Leon walked over and rested a hand on him, four fingers on the side of his neck and a fat thumb on his cheek. "You haven't answered my question, son. What's the real reason we're here?"

Slug gulped. His eyes turned to Karen for help, but she had her arms folded, a look on her face that said, *You better answer the fucking question, kid.*

His face quivered in Leon's hand. He closed his eyes and took a deep breath. "He said he'd kill me, man, I had to."

Leon's thumb slipped from Slug's cheek and onto his throat. He pressed gently. Slug coughed. "Had to what, Slug?"

"Leon!" Karen shouted.

Leon turned and saw that Karen had drawn her weapon and was aiming it above his head. He pushed Slug hard, sending him flying.

He drew his gun and spun around. "Hold it! Southeil P.D. Identify yourself!"

The lights that had lit up the walkway outside the upper-floor apartments had gone out, but there was enough moonlight to make out the ink-black figure of a man as it moved slowly toward the steps.

"Are you deaf?" Karen yelled. "Freeze and put your mother-fucking hands in the air. Now!"

The figure stopped at the top of the stairs and stepped out of the shadow into the white light.

Slug looked up at the man, tried to stagger to his feet but fell back on his ass.

Leon and Karen stood frozen in the firing position. They were unable to move as the man descended another three steps; they could only look on in horror, and awe.

The man was dressed in the typical random shit attire of a hard-done-by junkie: a long, rat-gnawed trench coat covered in cigarette burns and stains; a red sweater over a green turtle neck, the words World's Greatest Grandpa written on it; torn jeans pulled on over a pair of sweat pants. He wore one brown leather boot, one black. The black boot had no laces, secured instead with tightly wrapped duct tape. A faded rainbow-colored scarf was wrapped around the head-less stump of his neck.

"Wha—I don't," Leon said. He cleared his throat. "Slug, is that—,"

"Nikolis Cole," Slug whispered. He was standing behind Karen and peering over her shoulder.

A bottle in a brown paper bag dangled from between Cole's gloved fingers. He tapped it against the vertical bars of the railing as he walked down the stairs.

Leon was about to shout, "Freeze!", when a shot rang out.

Cole staggered back, slipped on the steps. He grabbed the railing and swung against the bars.

Leon turned to Karen just as she pulled the trigger a second time. The bottle in Cole's hand exploded in front of his stomach.

"I did what you said, man!" Slug yelled. He made a pathetic effort to push Karen to the ground. She cursed, spun around, and butted him with her pistol.

He groaned, falling to his knees. He raised his hands to his face. Blood leaked through his fingers. She grabbed the back of his head and mashed it into the ground, twisted his hands behind his back and cuffed his wrists. She straddled him as he squirmed and watched Leon throw himself at the decapitated junkie on the stairs.

CHAPTER SIX

Once Leon was on top of Cole, he panicked. There was no face to scream at, no nose to break, or head to knock unconscious. As he struggled with the cuffs on his belt, Cole's arm swung up, stabbing him in the ear with a bottle shard. He dragged the sharp glass through Leon's earlobe and down and across his face.

Leon screamed, fell back, and smacked his head on a concrete step. He was reaching for his head and his gun when Cole brought a heavy boot down on his crotch. Leon's eyes bulged from their sockets. He turned his head and threw up.

Karen leapt to her feet and emptied six bullets into Cole's chest as he grabbed each railing and heaved himself up. The bullets tore holes in his novelty sweater, but that was the extent of the trauma. He didn't fall; he had actually gotten to his feet. He turned and tilted his right shoulder toward Karen, as if to imply he was looking at her.

While he was distracted, Leon dragged himself down the stairs and onto the grass. He tried to blink away the blood in his right eye and tried to will away the nausea and dull ache that throbbed in his gut after the boot to his balls. He rolled onto his back, pushed himself up with his elbows. He reached a hand up and felt the sticky ribbons of flesh that were once his ear. He winced, pulled out his gun, and shot at Cole as he approached. Leon's eyes widened as Cole stepped closer with each bullet that entered his chest, almost as if the lead was fuelling him. By the time Cole was close enough to reach down and take the gun from his hands, it was clicking on empty.

Cole tossed Leon's gun in the grass, raised his fist in the air behind his back, and brought it down, punching *through* Leon's chest.

Karen cried out as she ran up and kicked Cole in his right pectoral with everything she had. Cole fell back, his fist pulling out of Leon's chest with a wet sucking sound. He was clutching Leon's still-beating heart.

Karen put her hands on Leon's cheeks as he exhaled his last breath. She closed his eyelids.

There was no time to mourn.

She ran just before Cole's outstretched hand could grab her leg. His fingers grasped at nothing, and a somehow disgruntled sounding gurgle came from the hole in his neck where his head had been severed.

Karen yanked Slug to his feet and dragged him behind her as she ran for the hole in the fence. She whipped out her phone, redialed, held it to her ear. All she heard was white noise.

CHAPTER SEVEN

"Karen, please, girl," Slug gasped. "Slow down, I'm gonna fall!"

Karen pulled the wire so hard that it came completely away from the post. She stepped through the gap where the flap had been and dragged Slug after her. She grasped his arms, held him in front of her. "Why, Slug?" she shouted, shaking him. "Why did you bring us here? Why does Cole want us dead?"

Slug's mouth opened and closed, opened and closed. He was mute with fear. Karen slapped him hard across the face.

"You better think of something to say by the time we get to the car."

As she looked out at the low rises, her eyes widened.

The lights were on in all the apartments and the occupants were gathering outside.

They were standing on the grass, leaning over the wall on the upper floor. Mostly teenagers, young boys, but there were a few elderly men and woman. Apart from a few children on the steps, looking down at Leon's corpse, everyone was watching as their Saint, Nikolis Cole, marched across the weedy square yard in pursuit.

Karen ran, hand on the small of Slug's back, pushing him ahead. They ran through the skate park, past the chop shop. They crossed the street to where the car should have been, but it wasn't there. Tiny pieces of shattered glass on the pavement winked in the moonlight.

She put her hands to her head and clutched her hair. "I don't fucking believe this!"

Slug smiled at her, a smile that didn't reach his eyes. "Shouldn't park your car here," he said. "It's a bad neighborhood."

Karen ran to the nearest house and started banging on the door yelling, "Police! This is an emergency! Open the door!" She ran to the next house, and the next, banging and yelling. "Police! Open the fucking door!"

Slug walked up beside her. He looked almost content, or resigned, when he said, "It wasn't a good kill."

Karen was gasping for breath. She squinted at him through a blur of sweat. "Wha—, what?"

She looked around at the windows on the street. They were all dark. She looked back to see if Cole was gaining, then something caught her eye. She could see a faint, orange flickering light through the holes in the chop shop garage door.

She grabbed Slug's arm. "Come on."

They ran across the street, and when she got to the metal door, she banged on it with her open hands. "Open up, police!"

She listened. No sound. She reached down, shoved her fingers in under the steel sectional door, and pulled up. She clenched her teeth, back arched, veins and neck muscles bulged. There was the sound of rusty metal scraping against metal, but it didn't budge. She let go and gasped for breath. She rubbed her fingers where the metal door had dug in and turned to Slug. "If you want to live, then give me a fucking hand!"

Slug hesitated, but then got to his knees. They both put their fingers under the door and pulled. Karen roared and the door flew open with a loud screech. She staggered and Slug fell on his back. They quickly got to their feet and hurried inside.

Karen turned and yanked the door down, surprised when it dropped like a guillotine with a loud clatter. She leaned her head against the wall, closed her eyes, and wiped sweat from her brow.

She opened her eyes and looked around. The light was coming from a barrel fire in the middle of the garage. There were a couple of filthy brown couch cushions on the floor, as well as a few tattered blankets. The concrete was strewn with crushed beer cans and liquor bottles, syringes, cigarette butts, and spent joints. There was a window and a door on the right that looked like it led into an office.

Slug was standing by the fire, rubbing his hands up and down his arms. There was a man curled up on the floor facing the wall. He didn't seem bothered by their intrusion; he just moaned and pulled his blanket more tightly around his shoulders.

Karen brought her hand up to her nose as she walked toward Slug. The place stank of urine and vomit. She glanced over at the toilet, a big, rectangular plastic bucket in the corner. She stood by the fire as she tried her phone again. Static. She cursed and was about to flip the phone shut when she heard a voice on the line, barely audible, the static still fizzing in the background.

"I know where you are," the voice said. The voice was husky and strained, like a non-smoker after taking a drag from a fat cigar. She turned away from Slug, hunched over, listening to the white noise. "Ol' Nik Cole knows what you did. Ol' Nik Cole is going to make you pay for what you did."

Karen's hand shook as she listened, waiting for Nikolis Cole to say more. But the Saint had said all he needed to say.

Karen closed the phone slowly and turned around. The man who had been asleep in the corner was now wide awake; he had one hand over Slug's mouth, the other holding a knife to his throat.

CHAPTER EIGHT

"Hey," Karen said, holding out her hands. "Easy, buddy. We're just here hiding out. We're not here to hurt you or to take any of your shit, alright."

The man's pupils were piss holes in the snow. His bearded face was covered in a hideous rash, his lips split with sores. He looked about fifty, but given he was a junkie and living rough, Karen knew he was probably closer to thirty.

Slug's eyes were watering, his voice muffled against the man's dirty hands.

"I ain't got no shit," the bearded man said. "You give me your shit. You gimme your shit or I cut open your boy!"

"Listen, okay," Karen said, reaching for her coat pocket. "I'm a cop."

"Don't do that. Don't do that. Keep your hands where I can see 'em."

Karen held her hands out in front of her again. "Okay," she said, "okay, but listen to me—"

"I ain't got no shit," he said. He took his hand away from Slug's face and scratched his cheek, nails digging in deep, flaking away dead skin. "You gimme your shit."

Slug gasped for air, then gulped when his throat touched the blade. His eyes were wide, staring at Karen, pleading for help.

She gave him a reassuring nod. "Buddy, I don't have anything to give you."

"You a cop," he said, sniffing, putting his hand over Slug's mouth again. "You got a gun. I could use a gun."

She shook her head. "I don't think so. Listen, we can—"

Slug's eyes widened in panic. *Watch out!*

Karen spun around and the woman behind her smashed a chunk of red brick into her face.

* * *

Karen woke up lying on her side on the floor. Her face was numb. She raised her hand and felt around. Her upper lip was split open, and she could feel her front teeth were hanging loose underneath. Her nose was broken. She ran her hand over her head and felt wetness weep from a split in her scalp.

The bitch had hit her in the head a couple of times with the brick, first in her face, then on the side of her head, knocking her out.

Where the hell did she come from, Karen thought. Then she remembered the office. She must have been asleep in there, or lying in wait.

She heard voices. Laughing. She looked around at the sideways world. Her vision was a blur. She closed her eyes tight, opened them again, and the world came into sharper focus.

She saw Slug. He was sitting on the floor against the barrel, holding his hands around the knife in his gut. His hands and shirt were drenched dark red. His eyes were opening and closing wearily, and he was breathing in shallow, rapid breaths. He was sitting in an expanding pool of his own blood. Karen was about to call his name when she thought of the voices.

She looked to the left and saw their attackers sitting on the couch cushions. The woman's hair was long and stuck together in clumps. Her face was shrivelled and her laughing mouth revealed rotten teeth. She was a meth head. She was leaning her head on her boyfriend's shoulder watching him play with Karen's gun. He had taken out the clip, was peering into the slot, trying to impress the lady by pretending he knew about guns. They were high, and they had taken the gun apart, but Karen still needed a weapon. She was in pretty bad shape.

She looked back at Slug, who was staring at her. He was crying, but silently. *Good boy,* Karen thought. *Don't make a sound. Let them think you're dead.*

Karen rolled onto her stomach and winced when she felt a stabbing pain between her shoulder blades. They must have hit her in the back when she was unconscious.

She crawled toward Slug, eyes on the junkies the whole time.

When she was close enough, she patted Slug's leg and looked at where he had been stabbed. It was bad. The knife was buried to the hilt and black blood was oozing from the wound. She looked him in the eye. "Slug," she whispered, "you're bleeding to death."

He nodded. He was pouring sweat and shivering.

"If I'm going to get you to a hospital I'm going to have to kill those fuckers, and to do that I'm going to need a weapon." She looked down at the knife in his belly and looked back up.

Slug grinned, took a deep breath, as deep as he could manage and whispered. "Get 'em."

Karen smiled back, put her hand on the knife handle, but then had a thought. She reached down and unbuckled her belt, slipped off her leather gun holster. She did up her belt and held the holster to Slug's mouth. He took it in his teeth and bit down hard.

"Try not to scream," she whispered. Her face was starting to ache and her head throbbed. She placed one hand over Slug's stomach and one hand on the knife and gently slid it out. A blob of black blood oozed after it. Slug spat out the holster; teeth marks had nearly torn through it. Karen had no time to ask if he was okay. If he was going to live, she needed to get him out of here, right now.

She jumped to her feet and ran. The woman looked up and screamed, raised her hand as the knife came slashing down. It pierced through her skeletal hand. Karen ripped the blade back out, and while the fan of blood spray was still in the air, she brought the knife down again, stabbing the wailing woman in the chest.

The man scuttled back on the floor. Karen turned to him as she put a foot on the meth head's chest and yanked out the knife. He let out a terrified moan as his shaky hands slipped the clip back into the gun. He raised it as Karen made for him, but he wasn't pointing it at her.

Karen was thrown sideways, hit the wall, then slid to the ground. She groaned in pain, watching through blurred eyes as Nikolis Cole walked past her and toward the junkie.

"I didn't think you were real, man," the junkie said, gun clicking as he pulled the trigger. He hadn't loaded it properly.

Cole reached down, clutched his upper arms, and lifted him above his headless shoulders.

"Please!" the junkie screamed. "Please! I'm a junkie, you meant to protect us, right? I one of your flock, right?"

Karen got up, feeling like she'd been kicked in the back by a horse. She ran hunched over to Slug, threw his arm over her shoulder, and helped him to his feet. His head rolled and rested against her face. He was passing out.

They made a quick shuffle for the door. Karen heard a splash and chanced a glance back. Cole had thrown the junkie into the blue bucket toilet and was holding his head under the vile soup of excrement that filled it.

CHAPTER NINE

They didn't get far. Slug was nearly unconscious and could no longer walk.

"Help!" she screamed out into the night, knowing nobody would answer. "Help, there's a boy dying out here!"

He was dead weight. She knew she couldn't carry him much further. She dragged him toward the nearest alley, thinking all they could do now was get off the street, hope that Cole doesn't find them, and keep an eye out for a passing patrol car. But she knew that wasn't good enough. The boy was dying. He'd be dead in minutes. She carried him down the alley and placed him against the wall behind a dumpster.

"Slug," she said, crouching over him, "can you hear me?" She gently slapped his face. "Slug!"

His eyes rolled open.

Karen reached behind him and unlocked his cuffs. She took off her coat. "Hold this against the wound." She took his hand, wrapped it around the sleeve of her coat, and pushed it down, pressing it against his stomach. She took her hand away and he held it there.

"I'm going to make a run for it, get help."

Slug shook his head and said in a slow drawl, "You'll never make it. No one's going to help us, and there's no running from Cole."

"Slug, we can't just lay down and die."

He laughed, then coughed blood. He wiped his lips. "Who said anything about layin' down?" he said. "I finally standin' up. I'm tired of runnin'. I'm tired of being afraid." He blinked. Tears ran down his face. He swallowed hard. "I brought you here, to Cole, because I was afraid. I don't like who I am, what I'm capable of, when I'm afraid. I just want it to be over."

Karen shook her head and stood up. "You're not thinking straight. I'm getting help. You're going to be okay, kid."

"It wasn't a good kill."

Karen looked out the mouth of the alley, then squatted, put a hand on Slug's shoulder, and looked into his eyes. "You said that before. What does it mean?"

He looked down, pulled the sleeve away from his wound, then pressed it back, wincing. His head fell back against the wall and he said, "You know what it means."

And then Karen realized that she did. She looked up at the moon, which was peering down from overhead, a spotlight shining down on a stage. *So bright,* she thought, before saying, "He told me the kid drew on him."

Slug reached up a shaky hand and took off his cap, ran fingers through his greasy hair, and followed her gaze. His eyes glistened in the light. "You knew," he said, nodding. "You knew that asshole better than anyone." He sniffed. "And I knew. I *saw*. We both saw, me and my friend, a kid named Charlie." He squeezed his cap in his hand. "Leon said he'd kill us both if we talked. Hell, I ain't no snitch anyhow, but Charlie … he wouldn't listen. I went to your partner and told him Charlie wanted to come clean." He shook his head, hair fell over his face. Black circles had formed around his eyes. "I told him I couldn't do nothin' about it. But he told me there was somethin' I could do. He gave me this vial, a fucking hotshot. I told him hell no, but he put a gun to my head, Karen." He put the fist clutching his cap up to his mouth and let out an agonized cry. "I killed my best friend, man, my only fucking friend."

Karen sat. There was no getting help for him now, she realized. These were the kid's final words and she was his priest. All she could do for him now was listen until he was no longer able to speak.

"Cole came for me that night," Slug continued. His hand fell away from his wound. "And I knew he had come for me like he had come for Zippo and his boys. I begged for my life. He held me against the wall." He put a hand to his throat. "Lifted me off the ground by my neck. Just before I blacked out I told him I'd bring you two to him, he could have you instead of me. When I woke up, he was gone. But I knew he'd be back. I knew he'd be back, and if I didn't have you to offer up he was gonna kill me. I did what I thought I had to. I did what I … I'm sorry."

Karen reached out and held his hand. "It's okay, kid."

"No," he said. He brushed his hair out of his face and pushed her away with no real strength. "I gotta pay the piper. I'm not gonna be afraid no more. I killed my best friend because I was afraid, and now I've gotten you killed, too. " He ran his palm down his face, wiping the wet of sweat, blood, and tears away. He smiled. "I'm sorry, Karen. I be seein' ya, girl."

He closed his eyes. His head fell. His smile remained. Karen checked his neck for a pulse. Slug was gone.

She stood up and turned to see the headless saint standing in the entrance to the alley. He wasn't advancing, so instead, Karen advanced toward him.

CHAPTER TEN

Karen stood in front of Cole. He turned and walked out onto the street. She followed.

Cole stopped in the middle of the road; his stance made it appear as if he was looking up at the sky. Karen looked around the deserted streets.

"They all know what's going down," she said. She looked around at the darkened windows. "Hell, those kids are probably back there poking my partner's corpse with a stick." Cole turned around. She took a step closer to him. "Why haven't we heard anything about you? Why haven't they told? Do they want to protect you? Or are they just afraid of the big headless monster?"

Her heart skipped a beat when Cole moved suddenly. He pulled his coat away from his frayed belt exposing an object clipped to his hip. It wasn't a gun; it was a small, battered grey radio, the kind that you charged up by turning a crank. She watched, puzzled, as he scanned through static, news, static, jazz, static, RnB, static ... He stopped at what seemed to be more dead air, then hooked it back on his belt.

"They are afraid," a deep, distant voice said, hard to hear amongst the white noise, "but they were afraid long before I died and returned as ... whatever it is that I am."

Karen realized that it was Nikolis Cole's voice speaking to her through the radio.

"I want to protect them," he said, hands moving expressively. "Make things better because it can be better. But they just won't stop destroying themselves, destroying each other. I can't stop the killing."

"If you stop killing people yourself, it might be a start."

He stepped forward. Karen didn't flinch.

"I killed them because they are part of the cycle of violence. I want to end that cycle."

"Why are you here?" Karen asked. She looked around. No sirens. No flashing lights. No one had called the cops. "Revenge. You some kind of vengeful spirit?"

The static crackled; the volume alternated between unbearably loud and inaudible.

"I'm no vengeful spirit. I'm here to protect them."

"A guardian angel, huh?" She spat on the ground. "My partner is dead. That boy is dead, because of you."

The phantom voice laughed. "I'm no Angel. If I wasn't damned, I know I'd be at Jesus' side right now. My sins are no less than any of the men I've killed."

"Then why not kill yourself?"

He seemed to consider this, walking around in a small circle, bringing a hand up to his non-existent chin. "Because I'm here for a reason," he said, holding out his hands. "Do you think this happens every day? A man with no head rises from the grave?"

Karen shrugged. "I've never left Southeil. Maybe in Europe."

"The answer is no," he said, not appreciating the attempt at humor. "So I must be here for a purpose. I am here to do something important."

"Murder?"

"Justice." He put his hands behind his back and began pacing back and forth. "I believe man's law has failed these people, so something brought me back to enforce a higher law, a more divine law." His shoulders turned to the low rises. "No one cares what happens down here." He turned back. "Hell, a demon has been prowling the streets slaying people out in the wide open and nobody knew. Nobody cared to know. Just a bunch of gangsters, hoppers, junkies, and hos, am I right?"

"I care what happens down here," Karen said. "Leon cared. And we're not the ones doing the killing. You're the one who ripped my partner's heart out of his chest. You're the fucking monster."

"That wasn't a heart." He shrugged. "That was just meat. The man had no heart."

Cole stopped pacing and turned toward her. "Your partner shot a ten-year-old boy in the face. The boy was handing over his gun, and he shot him. And do you know why he shot him?" The radio crackled. "Because he oinked at him like a pig. He was being a kid, and he got shot in the face for it. In the face, so the family couldn't even have an open casket at his funeral."

He took another step closer. Karen stepped back.

She felt sick. She had told herself to trust her partner, told herself that he wouldn't lie to her, that he wasn't capable of gunning down a child in cold blood, a child not much older than her own son. That's why she had lied. That's why she said she had seen the boy draw on her partner before Leon was forced to take the shot. That's why she didn't tell the truth, which was that she had been running behind them, and when she turned the corner onto that alley the boy was already dead.

But she knew what he had done, even if she denied it to herself. She knew because she was a good cop. She knew because she knew her partner.

Leon and Karen had worked a case once where a twelve-year-old boy had shot an eleven-year-old girl in the chest. When they spoke to the boy's mother, she told them that violence was a disease and her boy had gotten sick with it. Karen now knew that to be true. She had watched her partner become infected by violence, watched him succumb. She had helped him cover up a murder.

Cole was right. People didn't just rise from the grave every day; there must be a reason for all of this. Maybe Slug was right, too. Maybe it was time to pay the piper.

"So," Karen said, "you killed Leon, now you're going to kill me." She took a deep breath. "Fuck it." She exhaled. "I carry a gun to work every day, I've been preparing for this moment my whole damn life."

He walked forward until he was standing directly in front of her. The vacant space on his shoulders looked down at her, congealed blood oozing from the inside of his neck to plop on the asphalt. He seemed to pause in that position, and she waited for him to say something, to hand down his sentence. Eventually, he raised his forefinger. *One minute.* He took the radio off his belt, flipped the crank and began to turn it. Karen would have laughed her ass off if she wasn't sure she was about to die. After a minute, he returned the radio to his belt, which had crackled back to life and said, "I'm not going to kill you."

She waited for him to say something else. He didn't.

"Why?" she asked.

Cole unclipped her holster and slowly pulled out her gun. She didn't resist. He stood upright and pointed it at her head.

She stared down the barrel and said, "If that bastard did what you say, and I helped him get away with it ..." She closed her eyes. "Do it."

She listened to the white noise of background radiation, the sound of the beginning of the universe. She listened even though she knew she wouldn't hear the bang before the bullet entered her brain and killed her. She thought, for a moment, that she might already be dead, then she realized the dead don't think. She opened her eyes.

Cole leaned over, shoved the gun back in her holster, then stood back. "That's why," he said.

"What—what do you mean?"

She gasped when she thought she saw the outline of a face on Cole's shoulders, but then it was gone.

"You repented," he said. "You're willing to give up your own life for justice, justice for the ghost of a ten-year-old boy. That is the same higher form of justice I champion, an equal justice, above man's law. Pure justice." He stepped back. "Besides, you have a son. I don't want to risk creating another lost soul by taking a boy's mother away from him."

"But—but why do I deserve to live." She pointed her hand back at the alley. "Why did that boy deserve to die?"

Cole was quiet for a moment, except for the noise of the dead air on the radio. Finally, he said, "If the boy hadn't died, I would not have killed him. He repented. There is mercy for those that truly repent with an honest heart. But then again, if he wasn't dying, would he have repented at all? If that sinner hadn't stabbed him, perhaps he would not have asked for forgiveness, and I would have taken his life after all." He shrugged. "At least, with this death, and with his repentance, you can hope for his soul. Those who are removed from this earth by my hands have been judged unworthy of the gift of life; they are people that take that gift from others. You can be assured wherever I am sending them, it is somewhere where God's radiance does not shine."

Karen felt dizzy, weak; she held Cole's arm for support. She had forgotten she had been hit in the head with a brick, twice. She looked up and saw, more clearly this time, the face of an old man with a white beard and a white smile where there had been no face before. "But," she said, "I have to pay for what I've done. That boy was denied justice because of me."

"I won't kill you. The blood of your partner was justice enough."

"S—so, what," Karen said, slurring. "I learned my lesson, so now I'm free to go."

The voice on the radio laughed, and so did the old man's face, which was the silver color of moonlight.

"You don't get off that easy," he said. "A price must be paid for aligning yourself with a devil."

"An asshole," she said.

Karen looked over at the alley. Maybe it was true that Slug had to die tonight so that his soul could be saved, but she didn't think the kid deserved to bleed to death in an alley.

"At least," Cole said, as if reading her mind, "he wasn't alone."

She wiped away tears. "Did you know his name?"

Cole's torso nodded. "Kevin," he said.

"Kevin," she echoed softly. She turned around. "So, if you're not going to kill me, what happens now?"

He smiled. "You can think of it as a more lenient penalty for your crimes, but I'd prefer if you thought of it as more of a calling." He turned, facing down the length of the street. "I exist here." He walked down the street, away from Karen. The voice on the radio was getting thinner, lost in the static. "I am bound to this neighborhood. There are those that sin more greatly that I can't reach, beyond the low rises." His voice faded, and he was fading away, too. "Bring them to me," he said, even though he had dis-appeared completely. "Bring them here so true justice may be done."

CHAPTER ELEVEN

"Yo, Danny! What the hell's going on, man," Bel Shaitan said as the stretch Hummer pulled over. "What I tell you 'bout speedin'? I can't be getting pulled over by no five-o. I got hot shit in this ride, understand?"

"I understand, sir," the driver said, rolling down the window. "I wasn't speeding. Maybe we have a flat and the officer's just trying to help us out."

"Flat tire? Shiiit," Shaitan turned and watched as the cop stepped out of the unmarked car. He laughed. "Yo, we cool. It's only some bitch cop."

The driver leaned out the window and gave the cop a beaming smile.

"Evening, officer," he said, handing her his licence and registration.

She waved a hand. "That won't be necessary. I didn't pull you over for a driving infraction."

"Danny, what the fuck is this, man?" Shaitan moaned.

The driver cranked his head around. "The officer didn't pull me over for speeding, Mister Shaitan." He looked up at the cop and rolled his eyes. "Sorry," he said. "May I ask what this is about?"

She took out a wallet and flipped it open. The driver examined it closely.

"Karen Oswalt," she said. "Narcotics."

"Oh, wow," the driver said, holding up his hands. "I swear, officer, I've got nothing on me."

"I followed you here from the Harrow high rises. Mind telling me what you were doing in that neighborhood?"

The driver shrugged. "Yo, man, I don't wanna get in any trouble here. I bought the stretch a coupla months ago. My wife said I was stupid. I only just started picking up clients. Mister Shaitan here is my biggest yet, but only started driving him around the last couple of weeks."

"This the first time you've had to drive Mister Shaitan downtown?"

"Once, last week. Man, I don't like hanging around that part of town. Afraid I'm gonna get jacked, but gotta take the boss wherever he wants to go."

"Yo, officer!" Shaitan yelled, as he jumped out of the car and slammed the door.

He was wearing designer shades and a yellow Southeil Slickers basketball jersey.

Karen turned to him and held up her hand.

He stopped an inch from her palm.

"Excuse me, sir. I don't believe I asked you to exit the vehicle."

"Well I decided to exit the vehicle," he shouted, spraying a mist of spit on her hand. "Whatcha gonna do about it, you fuckin' ..." His voice trailed off as he clenched his ringed fingers into fists at his side.

"You fuckin'?" Karen asked with a smile. "Go on, Bel, give me a reason."

Shaitan stepped forward. "You fuckin' cunt bitch! I'm calling you a fuckin' cunt bitch, now what you gonna do about it, fuckin' cunt bitch? Huh? Whatcha gonna do? You know who I am? I'm Bel fuck-in' Shaitan, bitch!"

Karen's hand shot out, grabbed Shaitan's ear, and slammed his head against the roof of the Hummer.

Clutching his ear with both hands, Bel groaned as he slid to the ground. Karen put her arm around his neck and dug her knee into his back as she slapped the bracelets on him. She stood up and gave him a swift kick in the ribs.

"Arr, fuck!" he groaned. "You crazy bitch!"

"Officer," the driver said, waving her over. She stepped over Shaitan and leaned in the window.

"You might want to check the trunk." He winked.

"Thanks, Danny," Karen said, taking the keys from his hand.

"Actually," he said, looking out at Shaitan., who had staggered to his feet and was leaning against the Hummer. His ear was bleeding. "It's Devon. How hard is it to remember a brother's name, man?"

Shaitan grinned, revealing a mouth full of gold-plated teeth. He looked at Karen as she turned toward him. "Yo, I don't think this nigger knows just who the fuck it is he's talking to." His grin faded as he watched Karen walk past him toward the rear of the car. "Hey, whatcha doin', man?"

He turned to Devon, who grinned broadly and gave him a wave.

Karen opened the trunk door. She reached in and took out a black duffel bag.

"Wait," Shaitan said, stepping toward her with a trembling outstretched hand. "You need a warrant for that shit, man. This is bullshit!"

She pointed her gun in his face and unzipped the bag. "Back. The fuck. Off."

Bel Shaitan, who hadn't stared down the barrel of a gun in years, went weak at the knees and crumpled to the ground. Karen reached into the bag and took out two stacks of hundred dollar bills. The bag was filled with stacks just like them.

CHAPTER TWELVE

Karen pushed Bel Shaitan into the back of her unmarked car, gave him a little wave. She slammed the door and walked back to the limo, dragged the duffel bag off the roof and threw it in the trunk door, slamming it shut.

Devon was leaning out the window as she approached. She tossed the keys and he snatched them out of the air.

"Um, you're not taking my stretch are you, cos my wife will fucking kill me."

"Nope." She put a hand on the roof and watched a couple of cars pass by.

"Then, heh, shouldn't you be taking that bag of money with you?"

He moved over in his seat as Karen stuck her head in the window.

"It's yours," she said.

He laughed. "Excuse me?"

"You heard me. It's yours. On one condition."

"This is a joke."

"This is your motherfucking birthday, Devon. I'm serious, keep the money. I'm guessing there's anywhere between eight hundred grand and a million in that bag."

"Are you really a cop?"

Karen smiled. "I'm a cop, yeah, among other things. Take the money. You can pay off the limo. Keep your wife happy. Buy a house outside this God-forsaken city. Raise your kids somewhere away from ..." She glanced back at her car. "Away from the monsters."

Devon put his hand to his mouth, and when he drew it away, he was smiling. "Okay," he said, nodding. "Fuck it. Okay. What's the condition?"

"This is your limo, correct?"

"Yeah," he said, laughing. "Fucking dumb idea, huh, in this economy? Thought I'd won the lottery when I got a call from Bel Shaitan, big shot record producer, but the sonofabitch don't tip, not to mention, he's a grade-A fucking asshole."

"Tell me about it. So no one knows you picked him up today?"

Devon shrugged, still grinning. "Someone on his end maybe, just my wife on mine."

"Don't worry about his end, I doubt he told any of his friends at Bel Records where he was going today."

"So, the condition ..."

"You didn't pick up Shaitan today, and you never saw me."

He looked up at Karen, looking slightly unsure. "That's it?"

"That's it."

"And I can keep the money."

"Yes, Devon."

Devon nodded, then let out a shout and punched the roof. "Yeees!" he hissed, clenching fists. "Fucking thank you, Southeil P.D.!"

* * *

"What the hell is this, man? Where the fuck we goin'?"

The sun was low in the pink and orange horizon. A full moon was waking in the sky. A few grey clouds drifted overhead, and a shower of soft rain had started to fall.

Karen looked in the rear view mirror at Bel Shaitan. There was so much rage in his yellowish, bloodshot eyes that his eyeballs seemed to be trembling in their sockets.

"Why didn't you wait for the boys in blue?" he asked, fidgeting in his cuffs and looking out the window. "You just left all that money with Danny? You know how much was in that bag? You think Danny is going to wait around for the cops?" He laughed and let out an amused sigh. "Shit, I bet that nigger's halfway to Mexico by now."

Karen parked the car up on the curb outside the boarded-up chop shop.

Shaitan looked around.

"Where the hell are we?"

Karen got out, opened the back door, and dragged Shaitan out by the neck of his jersey.

"Yo, bitch!" he snapped. "You're rippin' my new threads."

She let go. The neck hole of his jersey was stretched out.

He looked down at his chest. "Yo, the Government gonna pay for this? Cost me a hundred dollars!" He looked up, squinted against the milky sun as it began to disappear over the horizon, looked a-round the street. "Where the fuck are we?"

"You don't know where we are?" Karen asked. "You should. This is your neighborhood." She shoved her hands in her pockets, looked down, kicked at the gravel. "Well, it was. Now it's *your* neigh-borhood, ain't that right?"

"Man, I have no idea what you're talking about."

She pointed up at the high rise. "You were over there visiting your old friends earlier today, collecting your percentage."

Shaitan looked up the height of the blocks. He opened his mouth to speak, then snapped it shut.

"Is that the extent of your involvement these days, Bel? Leave it to your Lieutenants to do the selling and the killing, and you pop downtown once a month to collect your respect money? Naah, I don't think so. I think you're more hands on. I think it still falls to you to decide who lives, and who dies."

He looked at her, his veiny head glistening with sweat. "This is bullshit, man. You've got nothin'. I'm not gonna do time for this. I'll be out in a day. And you know what I'm gonna do? I'm gonna come lookin' for you, bitch!"

She stepped toward him, took his arm, and led him into the skate park. "You've got a hell of a lawyer, I'll give you that" Karen agreed. Then she grinned. "That's why that corrupt motherfucker is next on my list."

"What the hell!" Shaitan said. "You crazy. What we even doin' down here?" His voice trembled. He pulled back as they approached the gap in the fence.

Karen put her hand on his back and pushed him ahead. He staggered, turned around. The anger had gone from eyes; now there was only a combination of bewilderment and fear.

"Don't worry, Bel," she said, pointing at her chest. "*I'm* not going to kill you."

"Damn, officer—" His voice caught in his throat when she raised her gun.

"Move."

* * *

He shuffled forward through the wet, freshly mown grass, looking around at all the faces watching him from the low rises. It was like a dream, the way their gaze followed him as he moved. Some were leaning against windows and freshly painted walls, whispering to each other. Others walked around the grass, kicking the ground, smoking, watching. The children watched; even as they ran around playing, squealing with laughter, they kept on casting expectant glances in his direction.

He stopped and fell to his knees. His shoulders shook and he began to sob. "Why, why, why?" he asked through the tears. He looked up as Karen walked in front of him. "Why are you doing this, man? I love these people. I give them jobs, I give them hope, a chance to make something of themselves. I'm a good man!"

"A good man wouldn't cry like a bitch," Karen said, shaking her head. "A good man would accept what he's done, and accept the consequences."

He put his fists up to his mouth. "Why are you doing this?" he hissed. He took his hands away from his face and raged, "Why do you suddenly give a shit what happens in this neighborhood?"

Karen knelt down and looked him in the eye, hands dangling between her legs. "I always gave a shit, Bel. Unfortunately, not enough people gave a shit. Why am I doing this?" She brushed her hair away from her face and looked up at the moon. "I'm doing this because where man's justice doesn't reach out, a higher justice will reach down. I brought you here because you are a predator, and predators are his prey." She looked around, smiled at a little girl in a pink dress spinning a hula hoop around her waist. Karen waved, turned back and said "And this is his jungle."

She got up, and when she walked away, Bel Shaitan saw what was standing behind her. The Devil of Southeil saw his final Judgement walking down the stairs and he screamed out in terror.

The full moon watched as pure justice was done down in the low rises.

GRAVE MARKER

SEBASTIAN BENDIX

ROCK, PAPER,
SCISSORS

CHAPTER ONE

"That was a total mess," Knot-top said. "We looked like shit out there."

Outside the van, snow was falling, forcing the grouchy guitar player to turn on the wipers. *It's fucking September,* Dreads thought, twisting a trademark dreadlock around her finger. *Every year this bullshit gets earlier and earlier.*

In the back seat, Weird Beard was drumming on his knees with some sticks. He was always drumming on his goddamn knees. You would think that it would improve his timing, but it didn't. If it were up to Dreads, they'd be looking for a new drummer, but it wasn't up to her. This was Knot-top's band, at least it was at present, and he was not going to give his best friend the boot just because he didn't meet the chick bass player's exacting standards.

But politics in the Filthy Habits were likely to change, especially since Dreads had become the focal point of the band. She knew she was hot, and it was only a matter of time before she leveraged that fact into getting her way.

"I thought we were pretty good," Weird Beard said, still drumming.

"You always say that," shot back Dreads.

"Hey, don't get down on me for being positive."

Dreads leaned back to meet eyes with the chrome-domed drummer. He smiled when she did, always with the same "Come at me, bitch" look that was part antagonism, part attraction. *I wonder if Joan Jett had to put up with this when she went solo,* Dreads considered bitterly. *Not fucking likely,* was her conclusion. If their upcoming independently produced debut album tanked, which in all likelihood it would, Dreads would definitely be putting effort into a solo career. She might even let Knot-top have a crack at the lead guitar spot if he could stop making sappy eyes at her every time she chatted up a cute guy between sets.

"Dude, you need to watch your fills," she scolded Weird Beard. "At least twice during the show, your transitions were totally off."

The drumming stopped. "My transitions are spot on. Maybe you need to worry less about sexing up your vocals and concentrate a little more on the bass."

"Her playing was fine," said Knot-top to the rescue. "Your fills were off."

"Bullshit," Weird Beard muttered under the tangled scrub of his facial hair. "Just hoping to get your dick wet."

"What was that?" Knot-top looked back to challenge him, taking his eyes off the rapidly snow-filling road. It was real nice that he felt the need to defend her honor, but Dreads was more concerned with getting back to the rehearsal space alive.

"He's just fucking with you," she cut in, hopefully diffusing the situation. Knot-top glanced to her, then back to the road, and they finished out the journey in silence.

When they arrived in the parking lot, there wasn't another vehicle in sight. The long utilitarian building that now housed Tactile Studios had been a thriving textile mill at the turn of the 20th century, back when this remote and sad upstate town had a reason to exist. But business had dried up by the 1960s, leaving the monstrous structure abandoned until it was purchased for cheap a few years back during the housing crisis. The sellers expected that the new owner would tear the building down to make way for condos or something, but the buyer, Chaz, was an aging trust-fund kid still nursing rock n' roll dreams. He renovated the top floor into rehearsal rooms to bring in some money and kept promising to put in a state-of-the-art recording studio on the ground floor—a promise that had yet to materialize. Regardless, the monthly rates were reasonable and the Filthy Habits had no complaints about the quality of their practice environment. But just looking at that boarded-up ground level gave Dreads a weird chill, like an untraceable wind crawling up her back— and she wasn't the type to get easily spooked. It kept her moving fast, even on hot summer nights, and it was only when they had all the gear loaded into the freight elevator that she felt any sense of relief.

A half an hour later and they were in the room, all the drums and amplifiers back in their respective places. Knot-top started rolling a joint and Dreads felt her annoyance grow at his stalling on giving her a ride home. Then she remembered there was no one waiting for her at home. Well, unless you counted a mother zonked out on prescription meds and vodka. The guitarist lit the joint, took a deep drag, and offered it to Dreads even though Weird Beard was holding out a greedy hand. What the hell. She took the joint.

"You know," Knot-top croaked through an exhaled cloud. "If we spent a little extra time working our material, people might be into us for something other than our looks."

Dreads took her hit and passed the joint to Beard. "What's that supposed to mean?"

"It means," Top continued, "that so far we're pretty much seen as an image band."

"According to who?" If Dreads were a porcupine, her quills would be bristling. "One of those skanks you bone?"

Weird Beard laughed, choking out pot smoke. "Burn."

Knot-top ignored him. "Whatever. I'm just cluing you in to people's perception of us." The joint cycled back around to his fingers. "Are you saying we couldn't benefit from a little extra practice?"

He had a point and Dreads knew it. She wasn't the kind of girl to spend long hours honing her songs—she liked the spontaneity of keeping the arrangements loose. But the truth was that their set wasn't getting any better, and her friends, when pressed, had all admitted that the band could be tighter. "Fine," she conceded. "We'll have longer practices."

"I'm down with that," Beard added, grasping again for the joint.

"You know," Top said, "that snow is supposed to get worse the next few hours. If we wanted to, we could pull an all-nighter and I bet the roads would be clear by the morning."

"Are you serious?" This sounded like the worst idea Dreads had ever heard. "We just got done playing a show. I'm fucking beat. I wanna go home."

"Yeah," Beard agreed. "I am kinda beat."

Knot-top smiled and pulled a baggy out of his pocket. There was no mystery as to its white, crystallized contents. "I can fix that."

Beard's eyes lit up and Dreads saw the rest of the night getting sucked right up her bandmates' noses. If she made a stink now, she'd never hear the end of it, so when it came time for her turn at the straw and mirror, she didn't resist. The truth was that she enjoyed the rush as much as either of them, and halfway through their first song the band had really locked into a groove. She looked over at Top as he wailed out a lead, really digging the sound he was getting out of his old Telecaster. Maybe this wasn't such a bad idea after all.

They were rounding the bend to the final chorus when everything suddenly went black. The amps sputtered out with a fizzling snort and Beard's drumming stumbled to a halt. For a stunned moment they sat there, swallowed by blackness and silence.

Beard stood up from behind his kit. "We blew a fuse."

Sighing, Dreads pulled her lighter from her pocket and went around the room lighting the candles that had been set about for the occasional "atmosphere"; i.e., playing while stoned. In the flickering light, their irritated faces made them look like angry phantoms emerging out of the dark.

"Someone's got to go change the fuse," Top pointed out cheer-lessly.

Dreads felt that unwelcome chill creep up the back of her neck. The fuse box was on the ground floor; the procedure for switching out the fuses had been explained to them when they signed the rental agreement. It seemed a lousy thing to leave in the hands of musicians, but the room was so cheap no one complained. Now Dreads wished that she had. Going down into that mill, so dark and foreboding, was something she wouldn't have asked of her worst enemy. But like Knot-top said, someone was going to have to do it.

"Any volunteers?" Dreads asked.

There were no takers.

In times like these, there was only one fair and determining so-lution—a game of Rock, Paper, Scissors. This tried-and-true tech-nique had been used to settle numerous band disputes, including food runs, driving duties, the loading of gear—you name it. This gave Dreads hope as she had an uncanny knack for winning, and the glum looks on her bandmates' faces told her that they expected this game to play out in her favor like so many other time before. Dreads, however, was feeling an unusual lack of confidence. Whether it was the drugs or something else, this night had her twisted up all wrong.

But she wasn't going to let the boys see it. "We doing this or what?" she challenged.

They dutifully gathered in a loose circle. Dreads nodded to Knot-top. "We'll do first round." He returned the nod with the understanding that the winner of this round would be out of the running and the loser would have to go on to challenge Beard for the unpleasant task. Both Dreads and Top held their fists to their chests, then looked to Weird Beard to do the countdown.

"Ready?" Beard asked. They were. "Once ... twice ... three ... shoot!"

Dreads looked down at her hand. She held her palm out flat, indicating paper. Her eyes moved to Knot-top's hand. Two fingers, extended. Scissors.

Scissors beat paper.

Dreads heart thrummed in her chest, syncopating with an invisible drummer. Even losing a single round was a rare occurrence for her, enough to give her an anxious jolt. Naturally she called for two out of three. Top rolled his eyes but accepted.

"Once ... twice ... three ... shoot!"

This time it was Dreads who put down scissors. But Top, anticipating the move, put down a closed fist—a rock. And rock beat scissors.

Now this ... *this* had never happened before. Dreads had never lost a game of Rock, Paper, Scissors, at least not against these two. She considered playing the chick card, using the excuse that there could be some rapist waiting down there in the dark, but she didn't want to foster the notion that she was some scared, weak, little girl. She wanted the boys to know that she was as tough as they were, so when the time came for her to take over as leader of the band, there would be no questioning it. If going down into a big spooky warehouse solidified that, so be it. But that didn't mean she was going to sign up for the job willingly.

Turning to Weird Beard, she readied for the next round, palm sweating inside her clenched fist. Top counted off, hands were thrown, and Dreads couldn't believe her eyes when she looked down to see that Beard had beaten her rock with his flat-palmed paper.

"Two out of three," she demanded again. Top counted off and the players threw down. Both of them scissors this time. They went again. Beard retreated back to his paper strategy, but Dreads held her ground, besting him with her two-fingered scissors.

"Last round," Top announced, his low drawl pitched up by the suspense. Dreads looked into Beard's eyes, sussing him out, trying to hear the dim rhythms of his mind. He returned with nothing, just a dead, unreadable stare, and Dreads made a silent plea to the universe for luck. *Please,* she asked the infinite cosmos, *please don't make me go down into that place. There's something horrible there in the dark, I know it. Please, I'll be a good girl ...*

"Once ... twice ... three ... shoot!"

It took a moment for Dreads to realize that she had shut her eyes, terrified to gaze upon the final verdict. But then Beard sighed in defeat and she knew that her rock had beaten his scissors. She opened her eyes to the welcome sight of victory and a warm rush of relief.

"Fine," Beard said. "I've been meaning to look around down there anyway."

"Yeah right," Top scoffed, poking a hole in his bravado. "Keep telling yourself that."

"Dude, you ever seen *Antiques Roadshow?* There's some serious shit in places like this.

The thought of Weird Beard watching *Antiques Roadshow* cracked Dreads and Knot-top right up, but the drummer waved them off like a couple of fools. "We'll see who's laughing when I score some crazy-ass sword brought over from Frankenstein's castle or some shit."

"Dude, all you're gonna find down there is some moldy yarn and a whole lot of rats," Top said dismissively. "But by all means, have at it."

After a moment's consideration, Beard opted to take his drumsticks along as weapons—just in case. As he headed out the door, Dreads advised, "Watch out for Frankenstein."

CHAPTER TWO

The ground floor was a nest of shadows, the only light being that of the moon peeking through the high-ceilinged windows. Several panes were broken due to punk-ass kids throwing rocks, but they were too high up for even the bravest vandal to attempt climbing in. Not that anyone in their right mind would want to. Beard took out his phone, turned on the flashlight app, and scanned the walls, looking for any sign of a light switch. He found one that looked to be at least fifty years old and was surprised when, after throwing it, a few hanging lamps sputtered to life, polka-dotting the vast space with pools of sickly light.

As predicted, the place was a scavenger's delight. Stacks upon stacks of antiquated textile equipment were piled all around, leaving little more than a hallway's width of space to maneuver at any given location. The closest comparative would be a junkyard, but instead of used cars there were rusted looms and knitting machines to get lost among. As Beard walked along the hulking stacks, he marveled at the old-timey craftsmanship; there didn't seem to be a piece of equipment here that dated far past 1950. He was tempted to dig into the stacks and see what he could salvage, but the jagged, rust-coated tangles of metal promised scratches and cuts and the certainty of tetanus. A trip to the doctor was something Beard couldn't afford, so he tabled his trash-picker impulses and set his mind on locating the damn fuse box.

He followed the snaking, archaic electrical system, finally finding the fuse box tucked behind a stack of old crates. The thing looked as though it hadn't been touched in decades; Chaz was apparently too lazy to set up a new electrical system. It took him a few minutes, but Beard figured out which fuse went to the Filthy Habits' room, and throwing the switch was satisfied that somewhere in the complex his bandmates were celebrating restored power. He could have just called or texted one of them to confirm, but Weird Beard just didn't operate that way. He was a man who did things first and worried about them later, if he worried at all.

His eyes now fully adjusted to the dim light, Beard caught a glimpse of an open door that led to a small, cluttered room tucked off to the side. An imposing physique and general attitude of reck-lessness gave Beard a cocksure edge, so wandering into the room was, for him, no great show of courage. But when he saw what stood there waiting for him, even his blind self-assurance was given a punch to the gut.

The first thing Beard noticed about the man was his shoes: black, outdated, and fastened with big brass buckles that were pol-ished to an impossible shine. His legs were long, freakishly so, and on his lanky frame he wore a tailored, pinstriped suit that was a garish shade of red, the sort of thing a carnival barker might wear. A stove-pipe hat sat cocked on his head at a jaunty, gravity-defying angle, and the hair that was tucked under it was shellacked and sculpted in a perfect, immobile wave. But the most unsettling thing was the man's face; his eyes, ice blue, were staring over a needle-sharp nose, and his mouth was frozen in a mocking leer. His teeth were small and perfectly chiseled, set in a gleaming row under blood-red lips. They were so perfect and white Beard figured they had to be false; no one had teeth that clean around here.

Beard tensed, expecting the man to charge at him, but then he recognized that this "man" was not a living human being but a tailor's mannequin—the largest he had ever seen. A wave of relief rushed over him and he laughed, feeling stupid for getting so spooked. He walked right up to the mannequin and stood there, looking up into the down-gazing face. The thing smiled back at him with pink plaster cheeks, painted to give the rosy illusion of life.

"What's up, dude?" Beard joked to the perpetually amused gentleman. Naturally, there was no response. Even up close, the manne-quin's appearance was quite impeccable; his suit was so clean it could have come straight from the dry cleaner's without a button missing, not a thread out of place. The only thing that seemed slightly incon-gruous was a yellowed piece of paper that was bobby-pinned to the suit's perfectly pressed lapels.

The words written on the paper were in an elegant script, as if drawn from the tip of a fountain pen. They were arranged in stanzas, like a song or a poem, and Weird Beard had to squint and get closer to read what they said.

CHAPTER THREE

Beard returned to the rehearsal room to find the lights back on, his mission a success. "Hey, check it out," he announced, holding up the paper he had found on the strange mannequin.

Dreads was grateful to have Beard back, as being alone with Knot-top always gave the room a weird tension; he always seemed ready to make yet another pass at her. She tried to get a better look at the paper the drummer was holding, but he held it away from her, teasing. Beard seemed to think that he and Dreads had some sort of playful rapport, but in truth she found him annoying. She didn't know which appealed to her less—his shaky drumming or his obnoxious personality.

An idea dawned in his low-watt bulb of a mind, and Beard grabbed a mic, adding wattage to his already loud voice. "Hold up, hold up," he shouted over the PA. "Give me some kind of riff. Something real dirty and mean."

Dreads looked to Top, who seemed irritated that Beard hadn't stayed gone longer. But he was willing to indulge the drummer so he shrugged into a snaky riff. Even Dreads had to admit that for an off-the-cuff jam it was pretty cool—hypnotic and spooky. She joined in, playing off of his root notes with a melody of her own, and soon they had a nice little loop going.

Beard bobbed his head along to the beat, digging the sound. After several measures, he held the paper in front of his face and recited into the mic:

> *Nothing good can ever come*
> *Of little boys who suck their thumbs*
> *To clean them up from head to hands*
> *We call upon the Scissor Man*
> *For the Tailor knows of parents' woes*
> *And with his shears clips filthy toes ...*

Before the grisly poem could be finished, blistering sound came out of nowhere, bulldozing right over the sound of their amplifiers. The Filthy Habits' jam imploded in a blast of feedback. Knot-top put down his guitar in a huff. "Fucking prog rock fucks!" he shouted into his mic.

The band renting the room next door was Delirium Tremens, a five-piece prog-rock band that had recently been signed to a major label, despite their music being nothing that any radio programmer would ever consider "commercial". They were partial to loud, droning jams that went on well into the wee hours of the morning, so the fact that they were drowning out the Filthy Habits at this late hour was not, in itself, a surprise. But it was odd that there had been no other cars in the lot, and no sounds in the hall to indicate the band's arrival, nor had there been any noises of instruments or amps warming up. There was just a blistering wall of sound that seemingly sprung out of nowhere, as if piped in from some deafening, prog-rocky dimension.

The mood was killed; there was no playing over that cacophony. Powerless to do anything about it, Top focused his frustration at Beard. "Dude, what the fuck was that shit you were reading?"

Beard showed the guitarist the paper. "I found it in the old mill. Freaky, huh?"

Knot-top snatched the paper, crumpled it up into a ball, and dropped it. "This is just bullshit poetry some Goth douchebag left lying around."

Beard scowled at him and picked up the paper, carefully uncrumpling it. "Dude, not cool. This shit is seriously old. I found it pinned to this creepy-ass mannequin down there. Trust me, no Goth kid would have the balls to go anywhere near that thing."

"What did it say," Dreads asked, strangely intrigued. "Something about a 'Scissor Man'?"

Beard gave the words a re-inspection at her request. "Yeah, I dunno. It sounds like if your kid is a dirty little shit you can call on this Tailor guy and he'll come take care of them with his scissors or something." His eyes glazed over a moment, lost in thought. "Maybe that crazy-ass mannequin was supposed to be this ... Tailor, come to think of it."

Just the thought of some creepy mannequin lurking downstairs gave Dreads the willies, and she was reminded of the disturbing German fairy tales her grandmother read to her when she was a little girl. There was something about a Tailor in one of those, who chased unruly children around with a giant pair of scissors. It must have been where the asshole who wrote that nasty little poem got the idea. Dreads never liked her grandmother very much.

"I'm gonna go have a smoke," she announced to the room.

"I'll go with you," Knot-top offered. But he didn't smoke, so this was some dumb notion he had of being chivalrous. Or he just wanted to hit on her again. Either way, gross.

"No, I'll be fine, thanks." She grabbed her leather jacket, checked to make sure her cigs were in there, and headed out the door.

Outside in the hall, Dreads stopped to listen, hoping to hear the prog rockers stop playing to talk or argue or do anything a normal band would do. But they just kept jamming; no stopping, no vocals, no comment. Those guys were weird, but tonight's sudden per-formance was off-putting even by their usual standards. They were into the whole bondage scene so it was probably an S&M sex-cult thing—maybe they were playing in a circle with ball-gags in their mouths or some crazy shit. Whatever the case, she had no interest in hearing it and was even less interested in seeing it, so she hurried down the hall towards the front of the building.

The lobby was dark and deserted, not that Dreads expected any-one to be there. It was usually Chaz manning the front desk, as he wasn't big on hiring help, and more often than not he was content to just collect the rent checks, stay home with a six pack, and let the tenants fend for themselves. And on a snowy night like this? Forget it. Chaz couldn't even be bothered to re-stock the ancient soda machine he picked up at a yard sale, let alone brave a blizzard for the sake of a lousy graveyard shift.

Dreads took her keys and her cigarettes out of her purse and went for the doors, but when she pushed up against them, she was met with firm resistance. She tried again, and again, but still the doors would not budge. Strange, as Chaz typically left the push-bar unlocked, not trusting the musicians to lock the doors behind them when they left. Taking a closer look at the bar, she saw that someone had jammed what appeared to be a knitting needle into the locking mechanism and bent it, creating a makeshift bolt. There was no opening the doors, not without the assistance of bolt cutters, and when Chaz saw this he would be fit to be tied. *He'd better not blame us for it,* Dreads thought bitterly, giving the jammed bar a final, angry shove.

She considered having a smoke in the lobby despite the prominent "NO SMOKING" sign, but then she remembered that the sprinkler system was new and Chaz had warned them that it was particularly sensitive. One whiff of smoke and the entire building would be showered with water, destroying all of the tenants' expensive electrical gear, including her own. Certainly not worth the risk of lighting up. She sighed, stowed her cigarette pack, and set off to find an exit that was not so inexplicably secured.

CHAPTER FOUR

Beard and Knot-top had attempted another jam, but the continued assault from the Tremens next door made it impossible. To drown his frustrations, Beard downed his beer, then felt an aching of protest in his already taxed bladder. He excused himself from Top, who could not have cared less, and hurried to the nearest men's room before he sprung a leak.

Rehearsal space bathrooms are notoriously grungy, and the ones at Tactile Studios were no exception. Despite being renovated only a few years ago, the single stall/adjacent urinal set-up had already been coated with an impressive layer of grime, and the areas that weren't filthy were either covered up by graffiti or band stickers that had already begun to wear off. But Beard had certainly seen worse—the dingy, two-bedroom apartment he shared with five other dudes wasn't exactly the picture of cleanliness, for example. Stepping over a puddle of unidentifiable liquid, he headed for the toilet stall but was distracted by his reflection in the marked-up mirror. Taking a quick detour, he checked his look in the mirror, and satisfied that his facial hair was having the desired wild-man effect, he doubled back to the stall.

The interior of the stall was somehow more disgusting than the outside, but it didn't stop Beard from dropping his pants and plopping his ample ass on the commode. Seated like a girl was his preferred pissing mode when he was alone and away from the judging eyes of others; it was relaxing, allowed him to think, and saved him the embarrassment of handling his unusually small penis. As his bladder emptied into the grimy bowl, Beard stared absently at the dull-witted graffiti scratched into the stall door, checking if anything had been added since the last time he sat here. Someone named Cheyenne was good for a rim job, apparently, and judging from her phone number, she was conveniently local. He was toying with the idea of calling her, just to be a wiseass, of course, when someone entered the bathroom.

All Beard could see through the narrow gap under the stall door was their shoes, but he immediately recognized them. They were those queer-ass Little Lord Fauntleroy numbers he saw earlier on that creepy mannequin downstairs; some hipster must have found the thing after he did and made off with the shoes, thinking they were cool, like for irony's sake. Weird Beard couldn't stand hipsters, especially ironic ones, and once, when Top had accused his beard of making him a hipster, Beard had almost knocked the guitarist's teeth out. His facial hair was an extension of his soul, and the notion that he might have grown it to be ironic was enough to spin him into a rage.

The shoes just stood there for several long seconds, facing in the direction of the stall, as if waiting for Beard to come out. When he didn't, they skipped across the scummy floor, *clickety clickety clack*, coming to stop at the yellowed porcelain sink. The faucet turned on with a rusty squeak and the wearer of the shoes stood there splashing water into the bowl for what felt like a full minute. *Wuss-bag*, Beard thought as he bitterly finished his pissing. *Probably one of those anal retentives afraid to get germs on his soft, girly hands.*

Wanting to give this douchebag a good scare, Beard hopped to his feet, pulled up his pants, then pushed open the door with a slam. He expected to find some dude in skinny jeans and one of those waxed, Salvador Dali moustaches plastered across his normally smug, now scared and stupefied face.

What he didn't expect to find was the Tailor.

The mannequin was standing with its back turned, facing the sink, its pink plaster hands held under the running faucet. In the re-flection of the mirror, Beard could see the thing's blank eyes staring at him, that ghastly frozen smile leering through the filth-streaked glass. Then, incredibly, one of the hands moved of its own accord and turned off the sink.

"What the fuck is this?" Beard demanded. The drummer felt his knees begin to buckle, and he put a trembling hand against the stall to steady himself. If this was some kind of joke, it was seriously not funny.

To the side of the sink was propped an item that took Beard's startled brain a moment to identify. It appeared to be twin swords—

sabers—that were bolted together at a pivot point where the hilts intersected. It soon became clear that they functioned as oversized scissors, a pair big enough to trim the nose hairs of a giant. Whatever their use, practical or otherwise, Beard did not wish to find out, so he stepped backward towards the bathroom door. As soon as he did, the mannequin spun to face him.

"Shit!" Beard shouted. "Do not fuck with me, man! I'm not playing!"

The Tailor wasn't playing either—or maybe he was; with that smile of his, it was hard to tell. With a lightning-fast move, he snatched up the scissors and held them outstretched like an elongated pair of hedge shears. Beard took another step back, but the Tailor matched him, giving the scissors a playful *snippety snap*. It was the sound of two razor-keen knives scraping together, and it gave Beard a rush of fear that crawled from his scrotum to his throat.

"Dude, I will seriously fuck your shit up!"

The Tailor didn't seem worried. He kept right on smiling.

"Fuck you, asswipe," Weird Beard concluded. He turned to the door —

— and the Tailor thrust out, skewering him through both lungs. The drummer tried to scream, but all that came out was a slow, deflating gasp, like air escaping a twice-popped balloon.

The Tailor rammed the scissors into the bathroom's cheap wooden door, shish-kabobbing his victim, a butterfly pinned to a display board. As Beard hung there, standing on tippy-toes, the Tailor pulled something shiny and sharp from his pocket. It was another pair of scissors, but these were normal sized, the kind used to trim fabric. As his life faded, Weird Beard heard the soft sound of snipping and felt his proudly cultivated facial hair fall away with the last of his consciousness. He hoped that in Rock n' Roll Heaven he might grow it back.

CHAPTER FIVE

There were two side exits in the complex, and Dreads had been to both of them. Like the front doors, she found them locked, apparently from the outside, and she dimly recalled Chaz saying something about keeping them secured after hours. So unless there was some other way out that she didn't know about, the band was trapped in the building until Chaz swung by in the morning to open up. The whole thing was totally inconvenient and undoubtedly a fire hazard, but Dreads was more alarmed about having to hold out for a cigarette than anything else.

She rounded the corner that lead to the Filthy Habits' room, hearing the racket of Delirium Tremens, and was passing by the doors to the men's bathroom when something caught her eye. Something sharp was jutting through the wood; it appeared to be the pointed tips of two large blades, and as Dreads drew closer she could swear that it was stained with blood. Despite instinct warning against it, she stopped to take a better look, and as soon as she did, the blades withdrew with the squeak of strained wood. Having seen enough, she was already hustling back to the room when the doors opened and two impossibly long legs stepped out.

Dreads naturally assumed that she was looking at some exceptionally tall and oddly dressed musician, one with a thing for stovepipe hats and freaking out girls with his grinning creep-face. But when the figure stepped towards her, it moved in a way that seemed entirely unnatural, as if it was a giant marionette brought to life by invisible strings. It was holding what appeared to be oversized scissors and was wiping the blades clean with an old-fashioned, frilly handkerchief. It didn't take a forensic scientist to identify the liquid as blood.

A body fell out of the bathroom behind the nightmarish dandy, hitting the hallway floor with a dull thud. Dead eyes stared at her, set into a face that it took her a moment to identify. Without his trademark beard, her drummer was nearly unrecognizable.

Blind instinct kicked in and Dreads turned and ran. Less than five seconds later, she was back inside the rehearsal room, slamming the door behind her, face white with shock.

Knot-top stood with his guitar slung at his waist, looking befuddled and a little annoyed. "Jeez. Where's the fire?"

Mindful that those blades might soon be stabbing through the door, Dreads stepped quickly away from it. "There's somebody out there. Some crazy motherfucker with a giant pair of scissors!"

"What the fuck are you talking about?"

Before she could explain, the volume increased in the next room, somehow more deafening than before. Like a coven trying to raise the Devil by the sheer power of their instruments.

Hell, maybe that's exactly what they had done.

Knot-top let his guitar hang to the side and went to see what was behind the door, but Dreads pulled him away. "Are you fucking stupid?" she shouted. "I just told you—"

Before she could finish, a single blade stabbed through the narrow gap between the door and the frame and started working its way around the deadbolt. That freakish thing outside was trying to jimmy the door loose, like a burglar breaking in with a crowbar. Dreads pulled Top with her into the center of the room, and they both looked on with fascinated horror as the blade jabbed and pried against the doorframe.

The music next door built to a thrum that shook the room, and it gave Dreads an idea born of desperation. She picked up her bass by the neck, and Top stood by slack-jawed as she slammed the instrument's body into the wall like a sledgehammer.

"What's that gonna accomplish?" Top shouted.

Dreads paid him no heed and swung again.

THWACK! THWACK! THWACK!

She battered the knock-off Mustang against the sound-insulated wall, hoping that the cheap building material would give before the neck of her bass did. A large dent began to form and a chunk of insulation fell, revealing the shoddy plaster wall underneath. A few more well-placed hits and she might make it through the bare wall, so she swung again as hard as she could ...

CRACK!

The neck snapped and the contoured, red-sparkled body of the bass fell to the floor, still tethered to the tuning pegs by heavy-gauge strings. Dreads felt a pang of loss for the instrument, but true mourning would have to wait until she escaped with her life. Unfortunately, the Mustang's sacrifice had been in vain as her blow had failed to break through the wall.

"Fuck it," she heard Top say behind her. He rushed past her, slamming his Telecaster into the dent she had started. Dreads was blown away that he would sacrifice his beloved guitar, but when she glanced back at the door, she knew why. The scissor blades were picking away at the wood around the bolt and soon the whole mechanism would pop right out of its housing.

Top was a wiry guy, but those arms had some muscle, and his swing did enough damage to put a crack in the wall. A few more blows and they could see the light from the other room.

There was a splintering sound as the blades cracked the door; it was only a matter of moments before the hideous mannequin would be inside, scissors ready to cut. Top dropped his battered guitar and went to the hole, pulling chunks of plaster from around the edges. Dreads joined in and soon there was a hole big enough for an average-sized rocker to climb through.

The room beyond was pulsing with alternating hues of blue, red, and yellow—someone's idea of a mood enhancer, no doubt. Under the circumstances, the psychedelia was an added layer of unwelcome insanity, but it was inarguably preferable to whatever was making Swiss cheese of the rehearsal room door.

"Ladies first," Top said, more urgent than chivalrous. He didn't have to ask twice. Dreads stepped through the hole, and no sooner had her Doc Marten planted down when she heard the splintering of wood and panicked arms pushed her the rest of the way. Her foot caught in a tangle of instrument cables and she stumbled, hair falling in front of her face as she wobbled.

When she righted herself and pushed back the dreadlocked curtain, what she saw in the room made her want to laugh and scream all at once.

Delirium Tremens were present and accounted for—at least their bodies were. They stood with or behind their instruments, the perfect wax museum simulacrum of a performing rock band. There was Butch, the drummer, ready to pound at the skins. Lenny on keys, fingers frozen mid-arpeggio. Even Dax (oh God, that name) was in his usual place at the microphone, double-necked Gibson SG riding high on his waist. Bass, lead guitar, newly added second synth player—they were all posed at their stations, looking ready to showcase for a manager or major label rep. The only hitch was that despite the music pumping out of the speakers, the musicians themselves were frozen in place, stiff as statues.

The music hit a chord change, the Delirium Tremens version of a middle-eight (more like a middle 48; their songs tended to go on and on and on), and Dax's arm moved suddenly with the change. But though he bobbed and swayed to the rhythm, his fingers remained frozen—in fact, they seemed to be coated in some sort of shiny glaze. Like nail polish. More of the band joined along; a strum here, a

drum hit there, and the casual observer might mistake their move-
ments for life. But the eyes—open wide, unmoving, staring
forward—as well as the lacquered, frozen faces—gave it away.

The Delirium Tremens were dead, bodies sealed inside some
freaky shellac.

"Jesus Christ," Top gasped behind her. Dreads would have
shared in his sentiment, but she was too busy trying to work out how
this twisted calliope was running. The pulsating light gleamed off of
thin wires that were attached to the players like puppet strings, pulling at limbs, left to right, up and down. The wire fed into eye-hole
screws fastened on the ceiling and led back to a strange contraption
that was fixed in the corner, behind Lenny, the keyboardist. It was
like a giant, old-timey music box with a crank handle and everything.
Some sick fuck had rigged this all up and set it to play just like an
automated Disney attraction; the *Country Bears Good Time Jamboree from
Hell.* The demented puppet master had even chosen a live jam ses-
sion of the Tremens to crank through the PA system, adding realism
to the ghoulish tableau. The more Dreads looked at it, the more she
feared she might crack and give up right there and then.

Fuck that noise!

Whoever—*whatever*—this thing was, she would not lie down and
let it make her its death-puppet. She would not go out like Delir-ium
Tremens.

Navigating the corpse-marionettes, Dreads bolted for the door,
grateful to find it unlocked. Top followed, and the two of them stumbled out into the hallway just as the scissor-man stuck his smiling,

shiny-smooth face in through the guitar-bashed hole.

"What in God's name is that thing?" Top asked, struggling to keep his grip on sanity.

"Like I fucking know." Dreads really wished he would shut up. She didn't want to waste valuable breath trying to parse through what little logic there was in this brain-boiling scenario. They just needed to get the fuck out of there, and fast.

When they came to the juncture that led to the front doors, Top naturally started in that direction, but Dreads grabbed him again by the arm, stopping him short. "Not that way," she said between tortured breaths. Damn cigarettes. "It's jammed shut. Probably by that thing."

Top sighed hopelessly. "Sweet merciful Christ."

"The other exits are locked, too. From the outside."

"Great. Just great." Top was on the verge of tears, ready to break. That would not be helpful. "Now what are we supposed to do?"

Down the hall, in the direction from which they just fled, came a snipping sound—the snapping of great shears. The Scissor Man was coming and Dreads was certain there would be no reasoning with him, no begging for a misspent life. "Look," she said harshly to her guitarist. "You do what you want, but I'm heading for the freight elevator."

The verbal slap seemed to do its job and Top pulled his shit together. He nodded in agreement with her plan and they ran past the juncture and into the roundabout maze of halls that would eventually lead them to the elevator. If they doubled back towards their room, they would reach it sooner, but there was the small problem of a scissor-wielding maniac blocking their way. Not that the circuitous route was a guarantee—there were at least three cross-hallways where the demonic freak could jump out at them, cutting them off at the pass before cutting them in half. But any chance, however small, was better than facing the hideous thing head-on.

Through the labyrinth they ran, taking every twist and corner like mice racing for the cheese. Coming to each cross-hall juncture was an exercise in heart-pounding dread, but their luck held out and nothing came at them from out of the darkness. By the time they reached the freight elevator, Dreads had reason to hope that they had shaken off their leering, well-tailored tormentor. But no sooner had they slammed the cage door shut when they heard the snapping of scissors, and then the mannequin was loping towards them, its legs taking impossible strides.

Knot-top punched the green button that, on a normal night, would have sent the elevator down to the ground floor. But because they were trapped in a real-life waking nightmare, nothing happened. *This is it*, Dreads thought. *We're fucked.*

There was a whir and a judder as the lift suddenly woke, likely stalled out from the earlier loss in power. Dreads and Top shared a grateful glance as the elevator started its shaky descent and watched as shiny, brass-buckled shoes ran at them across the slowly rising floor. Top had even managed a relieved smile when the blades shot down through the cage and speared him right between the neck and shoulder.

Dreads had never heard a man scream quite the way Top did at that moment; high and shrill, like a teenage girl. The Scissor Man's blades became wedged in the cage door, and for a second it seemed as though they would be trapped between floors. But rather than let the blades be ruined in the downward crush of the lift, the sadistic fucker withdrew the weapon, drawing a spark off the metal cage as the twin sabers retracted. Top collapsed to the floor and the Scissor Man watched, ever leering, as the lift sank beneath the floor and out of reach.

CHAPTER SIX

Once they were out of the freak's sight, Dreads rushed over to get a look at Top's wound. It was deep and bleeding heavily, but it was not, by her limited estimation, fatal.

"I'm fine," he said, reading her concern. "It's not that bad."

Dreads tore loose a piece of her already ripped tights, exposing a shapely calf. It gave Top a feeble smile and she wasn't about to deny a wounded man a little thrill. She wrapped the thin fabric over his skewered shoulder and under the arm twice, tying it into the most pathetic bandage either of them had ever seen. But it was better than nothing. The elevator clunked to a halt as they reached the ground level, and Dreads helped Top to his shaky feet.

The ground floor, with its piles of machinery and shadowy clusters of God knows what was just as unwelcoming as Dreads had imagined, but whatever lurked down here was child's play compared to what was coming for them, so she opened the cage door and stepped out into the shadows. Top followed behind her, close enough to touch, and the two of them made a quick scan of the cavernous floor with the hope of placing the exits.

"I'm pretty sure the main doors are that way," Top said, pointing to the far end of the mill with a wince. Dreads didn't have the greatest sense of direction, and the clutter didn't help, but she was reasonably certain that he was right. All that stood between them was a maze of textile equipment piled high to the ceiling and, more than likely, several species of rat.

And of course, soon, there would be the Scissor Man to contend with.

They made for the far side, claiming ground like soldiers through a battlefield, their eyes always forward. The maddening disorder of the place made a straight shot impossible, and several times they had to double back to work around an island of blockage. They had just about zigzagged their way to the midway point when the tap-dancing clatter of hard soles on cement came after them, like some demented Fred and Ginger routine.

"Oh God," Top gasped. "It's still coming after us."

Thank you, oh master of the obvious. But it did beg the question— what exactly *was* it that was chasing them? Was this some nutjob in a suit, bent on terrifying his victims before the inevitable kill? Did she have any old boyfriends that she had burned and might now be out for revenge? Or some band they had wronged? Club owner? A manager?

Or maybe this was some demon Weird Beard had summoned with that disturbing poem he found. The poem that was so much like the one her grandmother used to recite; the great tall Tailor and his nail-clipping, hair-trimming, child-torturing shears...

Her stomach sank. What other explanation was there? That creepy fucking poem had summoned this ... Tailor, or whatever it was, to dish out punishment to "unruly children"—and what children were more unruly than a rock band proclaiming themselves "The Filthy Habits"? Christ, their hair alone was enough to warrant the wrath of a demon obsessed with grooming.

Clack clack clack.

The sound of those shiny buckled shoes echoed throughout the mill, as if summoned by her thoughts. The Tailor was coming for them, coming to clip them clean with his shears, and he couldn't be swayed from his mission by pleading or reason. Their only hope now was to escape the mill and pray that once outside, their fastidious pursuer would be robbed of his invisible strings and give up the chase. They had to bet on the assumption that it was only in this horrible place that he held any power.

At last they came to the far end of the mill and two hearts broke in unison when they saw the massive pile of detritus that blocked off the doors. There was no getting over that pile, no digging through it before the Tailor reached them. They were totally trapped.

Clack clack clack.

The buckled shoes were getting closer.

"Jesus Christ, what are we supposed to do now?" Knot-top exhaled hopelessly. Dreads could feel the fight leaking out of him like water through a cracked fish tank.

But Dreads was not about to give up. Glancing around she saw that most avenues were blocked by the overwhelming clutter, but off to their right, about a hundred yards back towards the rear of the mill, was a warm sliver of light. That light indicated the presence of a room, and a room could mean windows, exits. It wasn't a guarantee, and doubling back could put them directly in the path of the Scissor Man, but right now it was looking like the best option available.

"Over there," she said to Top, grabbing his hand. "Come on."

Top's panic made him amenable, so he didn't offer any resistance. They wove their way carefully around the piles, listening for the hard-soled presence of their stalker. Twenty-odd yards from the room the sound of clacking shoes came out of nowhere, and they froze with their backs up against a hulking tower of machinery. The clacking stopped suddenly, a hound catching on a scent, and for a pulse-hammering moment it seemed certain that they had been detected. But then the shoes went skipping on their way in the opposite direction and Dreads and Top shared a silent sigh of relief.

Finally, they reached the source of the light, and it was, as guessed, a room. But the moment they stepped inside, it became apparent that whatever this room was, it would offer them no sanctuary, and certainly no escape. This was the Tailor's lair, a sewing room piled high with old looms, spinning wheels, and spindles of thread. And propped up neatly like a bizarre arrangement of scarecrows were several—five by Dreads' hasty count—mannequins. In this light, however, it was hard to determine if they weren't the bodies of the Tailor's victims, dressed in finery and displayed to his twisted, unknowable satisfaction.

One thing was for sure, Dreads had no intention of sticking around here long enough to find out. Still, there were sharp objects strewn about—knitting needles and such—that could possibly be used in self-defense. With every ghoulish revelation, it seemed less likely that there was a living being under the Tailor's suit, but if there was, a knitting needle in the chest would handle him nicely. Dreads freed herself from Knot-top's vise-grip and went to an antique table where several of the pointy implements sat waiting to be used.

Something rushed out of the shadows and Dreads froze, heart pounding like the kick-drum in a thrash band. Then she realized that the encroaching figure was only herself, or rather her reflection in a dusty, full-length mirror—the two-sided kind that pivoted on a free-standing hinge. The image gazing back at her wore a mask of anxiety so entrenched that Dreads could have sworn permanent worry lines had been added to her face. Guess she'd have the Tailor to thank if she didn't get carded anymore buying cigarettes. If she lived, that is.

She gathered the needles in a tight bundle and looked around for anything else that might serve as a weapon. There were plenty of avenues to explore if they had the time to look, but the blank-faced watchfulness of those God-knows-what mannequins only made her desire to get out of there more urgent. In the corner was propped a broom with old-fashioned straw whisks, the kind storybook witches rode. She grabbed it hastily and tossed it over to Top, who, despite his injured arm, caught it.

"What the hell am I supposed to do with this? Sweep him to death?"

Before Dreads could respond, a long shadow fell over Knot-top. He must have read the terrified look on her face because he craned his neck around like a condemned man sizing up the executioner's noose. The Tailor loomed over him, ducking his lanky frame through the low-hanging doorway. As Knot-top backed away from the advancing horror, Dreads could already see his knees begin to shake and buckle.

The Tailor lunged at Top with his scissors and the guitarist screamed and swatted back with the broom. They exchanged strikes and blocks in a puppet-show parody of a swordfight, the Scissor Man taking gleeful pleasure in Top's spirited defense, a cat toying with its prey. When he tired of the game, the Tailor began to snip away at the straw whisks, whittling the broom down to a nub. Sensing the inevitable, Top hauled back and whacked the mannequin hard across the face with the broom handle, causing the plaster to splinter and crack. A piece of the Scissor Man's lower lip fell to the floor, leaving his face in a lopsided half-leer/half-frown.

And with this offense, the Tailor was through playing around. He snapped the blades shut just above Knot-top's hairline, scalping him with one snip. The guitarist's skull cap spilled to the floor, along with a chunk of his brain and the knotted clump of his hair.

Seeing her friend fall gave Dreads an adrenalized rush of courage, and she charged at the Tailor with the knitting-needle bundle. He regarded her with a bemused interest (or was it a trick of the light?), withdrawing the blades from Top's body, allowing it to slide lifelessly to the floor. Dreads slammed the needles into the Scissor Man's chest, right above his breast pocket, but the fucker did not so much as flinch. She pulled the bundle out, but it wasn't blood that poured from the ragged hole in the mannequin's chest; it was sawdust.

"For fuck's sake," Dreads gasped as she stumbled back. The Tailor looked down at the hole, and the light played tricks on his face, changing his leer to a frown of disgust. Dreads watched in stunned fascination as the mannequin put down the shears, reached into a pocket, and produced a patch of fabric to put over the "wound". Then the freak produced a needle and thread and, with blinding, unnatural speed, stitched himself up. The job was nearly finished by the time Dreads snapped out of her daze and ran.

She hadn't even reached the elevators before she could tell they would be of no use; the controls had been damaged, hacked to pieces by the Scissor Man's shears. She doubled back into the labyrinth of textile equipment, scrambling off in a random direction, desperate to find any crawlspace, nook, or bin in which she might hide. In all her life, she had never lived more in the moment than she was right now. Forget all the plans, ambitions, and dreams of the future. All that mattered now was the simple act of staying alive.

By the third dead end, Dreads concluded that if she were going to survive the night she would have to find a way to turn the tables on her scissor-wielding tormentor. But how to stop a thing that didn't know pain and couldn't be injured? How do you kill something that never had life—at least not in any sense that logic could explain—to begin with?

Frustrated, she kicked a looming tower of junk, and when it

wobbled, unstable, she was struck with an idea. Maybe she didn't have to kill the thing. Maybe she could trap it for a while, long enough to find a way out of this miserable place. Once outside, she was certain that it all would be over—there was no way that thing was going to come after her in broad daylight, in full view of the waking, rational world. The Tailor was a nightmare, and nightmares only existed in the realms of darkness and shadow. Dreads truly believed that if she could make it outside, into the daylight, she would be free of the Scissor Man forever.

Somewhere in the maze of debris the clacking heels drew closer, honing in on her like a tap-dancing missile. "Come and get me," Dreads said with defiance as she squeezed into a gap behind the teetering junk tower and another smaller pile. "I'm right here, you bastard."

Clack clack clack.

The shoes approached and skidded to a stop. By Dreads' estimation, they were standing directly on the other side of the tower, waiting for her to reveal herself with a movement or a sound. *Oh, I'll give you a sound alright.* Bracing her back against the smaller pile, she planted her boots on the rusty barrel that anchored the junk tower and pushed with all the strength her compact little body could muster.

The tower fell, crashing all around in a deafening clatter, a bashing symphony of metal. Dust that had collected for the better part of a century plumed from the wreckage like a volcanic cloud, blotting out everything with a swirl of grey filth. Dreads covered her mouth, holding her breath, desperate not to take the contaminated air into her lungs. As the dust began to settle, she scanned the area for signs of the killer, but all she could make out were vague, twisted shapes in the haze. Nothing moved, giving her reason to hope. She drew a gasp of stale air...

The mote curtain descended, and there, standing beyond the pile, was the Scissor Man, shears still clutched in his grip. Dreads' heart fell into her stomach and she nearly followed it to her knees, ready to beg or cry or try to reason with the giant, living marionette. But the Tailor did not move. He just stood there, still as stone, painted eyes looking warily down at the filthy pile of refuse that blocked his way.

Somehow this angered Dreads the most, short circuiting her terror. It wasn't enough for this Devil's plaything to murder her, he had to make a toy of her as well? Not enough to take her band, take all that mattered to her—now the fucker wanted to play games? "What are you waiting for?" she cried at the thing. "Just do it already! Just kill me!"

In a show of defiance, she kicked at the pile, freeing a whole new cloud of dust onto the Tailor. The mannequin reeled back in terror, dropped the shears, and held up a hand to shield his face from the incoming dust. But it was too late. The fiend's smiling plaster visage was coated in filth, soiling the pristine, pinkish flesh tone to a sickly greenish-brown.

Like a stuntman doing a fire gag, the Tailor stumbled and thrashed about. It was as if the dirt was poison to the freak; Dreads was reminded of the Wicked Witch in *The Wizard of Oz* and her weakness to water—only this was the exact opposite. Going with that theory, she scooped a handful of dirt up off the floor and threw the choking cloud into the mannequin's face.

The Tailor stumbled back into a pile of debris, snagging his once-pristine jacket on a jagged hook of unidentified junk. Not waiting for the thing to free himself, Dreads charged, scooping more dirt off the floor as she ran. "Eat shit," she hissed, throwing the dust and debris into the Tailor's already soiled face. The fiend thrashed and hitched with revulsion, making Dreads all too eager to do it again. So she did. And she did it some more. She threw so much filth at the freakish thing that the dust-laden air invaded her lungs and forced her over into a coughing fit. Looking down at the floor, she found that in her frenzy she had all but swept it clean.

Through the settling dust, she kept her eye on the Tailor. The nightmare man sat in the wreckage, coated in filth, clipped of whatever invisible strings gave him life. Dreads stood there, watching for any movement, any sign of re-animation. But the Tailor did not move.

A dry chuckle rose in her tortured throat. She had done it. She had beaten the fucker.

Picking the giant scissors off of the floor, she rammed them into the mannequin's chest. Then she backed away, leaving them stuck there as sawdust poured out in a slow trickle.

"How do you like it, asshole?"

The Tailor did not answer.

The only thing that could make this moment sweeter was a smoke. Reaching into her jacket pocket, she found the soft pack there, crumpled next to a small pink lighter. Most of the cigarettes were broken, but sorting through them, she managed to tap one out that was only somewhat bent. Totally smokeable. She popped the cancer stick into her mouth, lit the tip until it grew into a tiny fireball, and dragged deep. Never, in all her years as a smoker, had a single cigarette ever tasted so good.

She hadn't even thought of the sprinkler system until the fire alarm went off.

Startled, she rose to her feet and laughed when she realized what she had done. The loss of her gear was the least of her worries at this point, but still she stamped out the butt, hoping a shower could be avoided. A sudden spatter of drops landed on her nappy head and she knew that it was too late. She was still laughing when the sprinklers—the only semi-modern fixtures in this museum of useless antiques—sprayed down water.

Dreads gave herself over to the moment, allowing the indoor rainstorm to cleanse her. She felt the dust and filth wash from her body, taking with it the horror of the last few hours. Raising her arms, she looked towards the ceiling, as if to the heavens. Water streamed down her face, tears of joy, the cold shock of the shower restoring her soul. It was a rock n' roll baptism.

There was the scraping of metal, the movement of debris, and Dreads spun around just in time to witness the Scissor Man rising from the junk pile. She watched with sinking dread as a long arm snaked around and pulled the shears free from a mannequin chest, spilling out sawdust with a dry squeak. The water had cleansed the Tailor as well, freeing him from the binding spell of filth; face restored to a rosy pink sheen, eyes gleaming with a water-washed shine, moving with smooth, renewed purpose. All that was left to do now was to run.

Dreads didn't even realize she had run into the sewing room; all semblance of reason had abandoned her as soon as the scissors had resumed their *snappity-snap*. Some dim part of her hoped that she could barricade herself in the cluttered room and hold out until the light of day drove the demon away—but there was no sanctuary to be found amongst the spindles of thread and spinning wheels. De-spair hitching in her throat, Dreads stumbled towards the free-stand-ing mirror, seeing the finality of defeat etched permanently on her once-bold and pretty face. There was a whistling sound behind her, a javelin tossed through the air, and something struck her back with such force that it propelled her into the mirror. Her head hit the glass, cracking it, and she felt the cold length of the shears running through her insides.

As she hung there, pinned to the mirror, Dreads watched her reflection in the spider-webbed cracks of the glass. Then came the shoes, that jaunty, skipping, *clickety clickety-clack*, and the leering Tailor arrived for one final grooming. The last thing Dreads was aware of before she died was the snipping of small scissors and the soft pad of dreadlocks hitting the floor.

CHAPTER SEVEN

After some trouble starting his jeep, Chaz arrived at Tactile around eleven the next morning and dutifully went about prying the sewing needles out of the locks. Clean-up days were always the worst; it was comparable to the hungover salvaging of a messy house after an all-night rager. But it was worth it to get back at these full-of themselves pricks, prancing around him with their slick, Japanese guitars and effortlessly shaggy haircuts. Chaz hadn't had any hair since he was thirty years old, the same year his band broke up and his rock dreams died. He was living a different dream now. This dream didn't come with fanfare, and certainly not groupies, but there was satisfaction in it, creativity even. Maybe it wasn't blasting power chords through a Marshall stack, but having your own murderous golem to puppetmaster wasn't too shabby a consolation.

After a quick tour of the rooms (he was both impressed and irritated that the Filthy Habits had managed to smash through the wall), he went down to the mill to check out the rest of the damage. The Tailor was back in his place of repose, leering blankly, waiting patiently for his next conjuring, his next call to kill. Knot-Top lay there where the Scissor Man had scalped him, brains on the floor, hair looking like the chopped-off top of a coconut. Only this coconut had a ponytail on top. That was going to be a bitch to get looking right.

Then he looked over and saw Dreads, still standing, shears pinning her like a butterfly on a display board. Even shorn of her locks she was achingly beautiful. She was to be the prize of his collection, the crowning jewel in his next mechanized minstrel show. At last, under his careful supervision, she would finally be a star.

He couldn't wait to get started.

EPILOGUE

"And that was it," Shockhead said to the stunned, heavily mascara'd faces of his bandmates. "No bodies were ever found. The Filthy Habits literally disappeared off the face of the earth. They even left their gear behind and everything."

Faux-hawk shivered behind his synth rig. "Jesus. And they practiced here? At Tactile?"

Shockhead nodded. "Yup. You know that wing down the hall Chaz is renovating? I guess their room was over there. He says they totally trashed it, busted a hole in the wall and everything. Almost as if they were trying to escape."

The other musicians exchanged uneasy glances. Shockhead reveled in the effect that the story was having. Sure, it was just a bunch of nonsense he heard being passed around the clubs, but who didn't enjoy a good ghost story? Aside from his new bandmates, that is. For a Goth group, the Dire Needs were surprisingly easy to spook. Pussies.

The door slammed open and Half-shave stood there, a piece of yellowed paper clutched in his hand. "Dudes," he said excitedly. "The ground floor is totally sick! You gotta check out this crazy thing that I found."

Half-shave closed the door behind him and went to the mic, paper in hand.

JOSHUA REX

COATTAILS

CHAPTER ONE

The store was three creaky levels of antiques and overpriced vintage junk stuffed into a series of small rooms. Julie stood in the stuffy basement level, breathing that musty uniform scent of the past while perusing the bric-a-brac and ephemera for a birthday gift for Ryan. There seemed to be no order to the clutter. A row of rotary phones stood atop a paisley ironing board. A couch with cat-shredded upholstery slouched in front of a curio cabinet filled with fast-food toys standing on doilies. In a corner of the room, Julie glimpsed a milk crate of old LPs. Ryan loved vinyl. She thumbed through the records but didn't recognize any of the names. Beside the crate stood a stack of cardboard-backed concert posters. She sorted through these next, the dry, crinkly protective plastic coming off in yellowed flakes that fell to the floor, but again found nothing of interest. The stack was partially recessed into a niche in the wall, and as she flipped the last poster, she saw something at the back of the alcove—a coat and tails draped over the shoulders of a female mannequin. An arm jutted out from under one of the black lapels, reaching out towards her with a discolored hand that was missing fingers.

Julie lifted a cuff and inspected it. The coat was wool, matted down and brownish tinged, but still pliable despite its age. She slid her fingers along the seam of one of the sleeves. Thick, black thread held the parts together and the intricately engraved buttons on. *Quality,* she thought as she stood back and sized it up. The shoulders were too slight for Ryan's boxy build, the waist too narrow, and the thought of the tails hanging around his shredded jeans made her laugh.

No way.

Nevertheless, she took the coat off the mannequin and held it up by the neckline. If felt strangely weighty.

Too heavy, said a small voice in her mind. *But it's wool … wool is heavy.*

She laid the coat on top of the records, ran her fingers down its velvety lapels, and opened the panels. There was no maker's tag—not even a price tag. The lining was silky and wrinkled and covered with large, brown stains. It smelled musty, but also distantly foul.

Of course it smells. It's probably a hundred and fifty years old. Just needs to be dry cleaned. It's well made. Hard to find quality like this these days. It will fit him. And if it doesn't, he can have it altered. It's well made …

Julie draped it over her arm and went upstairs to the pay. The clerk was a tall, doughy man with a protruding belly and a graying goatee. She set the coat on the glass checkout counter next to the grimy cash register. His eyes paused on her breasts on their way down to the coat.

"I don't think it's your style."

"It's for my boyfriend," said Julie.

The clerk raised an eyebrow. "He's going to wear it, huh?"

"That's the idea."

"He must be a *small* guy."

Julie gave him an irritated glance. "How much is it?"

He flipped the coat over, checking for the price tag. When he didn't find one, he looked up at her and frowned

"What happened to the tag?"

Julie shrugged. "There wasn't one."

"I find that hard to believe."

"Well, I didn't rip it off."

"I'm not saying you did. It's just that I'm militant about tags around here ..." He kept searching for it, his brow bent like crows' wings. "Actually, I don't remember this piece. Could be a consignment. What room was it in?"

"The basement. Hanging on a mannequin behind some posters," said Julie. This appeared to only further mystify him. He looked up, squinting as he mentally scanned the shop inventory in his mind. Julie tapped her fingernail on the glass counter impatiently. "So ... how much?"

"Well, Mondays are fifty percent off clothing. If it had a tag, it would say one-ten."

"So fifty-five then?"

The clerk gave a curt nod and rang up the sale without another word. She knew he'd go hunting for that lost tag as soon as she left.

He stuffed the coat into a flimsy paper bag and handed it to her without a "Thank you, please come again."

CHAPTER TWO

Julie walked to the bus stop holding the package against her chest. It was a blustery, late-fall evening, and although it was only five o'clock, the sun had already set. She waited in the little kiosk with a few somber-faced commuters and silently shuffled on the bus along with the rest of them when it arrived.

Including all the stops, it was a thirty-minute ride to Ryan's, and by the time the bus reached his neighborhood, it was packed and smelly. As they were going through an intersection, a black SUV ran a red light. The bus driver slammed on the brakes, missing the gas guzzler by inches. Passengers standing in the aisle fell into each other like dominoes. Julie, in an aisle seat, hit her head on a metal pole in front of her and the bag flew from her lap, spilling the coat onto the floor. Dazed, she slid off the seat and was gathering it when she saw a face looking at her through the legs.

It was a man's face, pallid and gaunt, with eyes the color of swamp weed and a thicket of black hair streaked with large grey patches. It hovered at knee-level, staring at her with an expression both comedic and sinister. The bus made a sudden sharp turn and the crowd shifted with the motion, obscuring the face. Julie bent her head to keep it in view as the bus righted its course and the forest of legs moved back to their previous position, but she didn't see it again. She settled back into her seat and tried to stuff the coat back into the paper sack, but it tore down the front. Julie cursed under her breath. She refolded the coat and, after much finagling, managed to get it back in the bag, all the while searching the heads around her for that strange leer.

Ryan's stop came and she got off. As the bus drove away, she looked up at the smeary windows, hoping to see the face again, but all she saw was a crude word written on the fogged glass.

CHAPTER THREE

Ryan had just moved into an apartment on the second floor of a freshly renovated Victorian in a wealthy area of the city. The price of the place had been insanely inflated, but Ryan—existing on a lifeline of cash from his stock market-savvy parents—hadn't needed to consider that. For them, money served as a proxy for love.

Julie had considered it, though. Every time she walked down the flagstone sidewalks, every time she passed under the giant, gnarled arms of ancient oaks lining the brick streets along which stood the grand, old houses built during the city's heyday, she was reminded of the different paths on which they'd come to the university.

Ryan had been a lethargic underachiever, more interested in guitars than grammar. He'd floated in on mediocre grades (which he continued to earn two years into the program). Julie had earned a full scholarship to the school's nursing program after four years of high school college prep courses. Her mother, a widow since Julie was three, worked the graveyard shift at a meat-packing plant and shoveled her own driveway in the winter.

Yes, different paths, Julie thought. *But I'd marry him in a second.*

The street lamps cast murky yellow orbs on the dark grey façade of the house. Light beamed from the second-floor bay windows and the bulb over the entrance glowed like the rear end of a firefly. Julie used her key to the outside door, climbed the creaky wooden stairs, and went through the apartment door, the bottom skidding along the new living room carpet. Rock music echoed through the half-empty house. Everything was white—the walls, the doors, the trim, even the old radiators that hissed and popped and crackled as if protesting the renovations. A futon—still in the same spot the movers had left it the week he'd moved in—stood against the opposite wall, still in "bed" mode from the previous night.

Julie snaked through the maze of unpacked boxes and went into the kitchen. Ryan was sitting on the floor next to the table, flipping through a celebrity magazine and devouring a slice of pizza. The box was open and half the pie was gone. A little radio on the table top next to more boxes blasted tunes into the room. Julie set the package on the counter and joined him on the floor.

"Why don't you eat at the table like a normal human?"

"There's boxes on it," said Ryan with his mouth full. His clear green eyes shone beneath the overhead fluorescent lights. He swallowed, then wrapped an arm around her waist. She bent and kissed him.

"Are you hungry?"

"Starving," said Julie.

Ryan snatched a paper plate from the table top, took a slice from the box, and served it to her as if he'd just prepared some rare culinary delight. She smiled and took a bite.

"What's in the package?"

"Your birthday present."

"Oooh! Can I open it now?"

"Not until tomorrow! Besides, it's not even wrapped."

"But it's almost open already. I can see it's clothes."

Julie looked at the torn bag and sighed. "Alright, I suppose."

Ryan grabbed the package, a big grin on his round, stubbled face, and sat on the edge of the table. He play-poked at the bag, as if guessing what it could be, and as she watched him, it occurred to Julie how strange a gift it was. In fact, now it seemed the *wrong* gift entirely. Why had she bought it in the first place? She couldn't recall deciding to, and now she wanted to take it back just to get it out of the house.

But Ryan had already pulled the coat from the scrap of a bag and was holding it up and looking at it with a confused expression. The coat looked comically small in his big hands, and shabbier in the plain bright light. The tails were stiff and discolored. Wiry, bent threads stuck up from the shoulders like ugly black hairs. Ryan's eyes moved over it, his brow wrinkling, then relaxing and wrinkling again. He rubbed the material between his fingers, sniffed it, then quickly held it away, like an animal backing away from something dead.

"I'm sorry, Ryan. This is the stupidest gift ever."

"What do you mean?"

"This smelly, raggedy thing that's supposed to pass for a birthday present."

"It's not raggedy," he said, scrutinizing one of the buttons with the focus of an archaeologist sweeping dust away from a fascinating new find. "It's *amazing*. I mean just *look* at it. It looks like it belongs in a museum. It's so ... *well made*."

Julie frowned. "It's in really bad shape. It didn't look this rough in the shop."

"What shop?"

"Some vintage place on the west side." Julie reached for the coat. "Seriously, I'm returning it."

"No way," he said, pulling it away from her.

"What are you going to do with it?"

"Wear it."

"You can't wear it. There's no way it's going to fit."

"Let's see," he said, as he swung the coat up over his shoulders. Julie didn't try to stop him. She thought watching him try to stuff his thick arms into the slender sleeves would make for a humorous piece of dinner theater.

But then he *was* wearing it, and not only did it fit well—it fit *perfectly*—as if it had been tailor made for him. The shoulders were no longer slight and angled, but square, shaped to accommodate his own; the waist contoured so that when he pulled the panels around his chest, the buttons found their holes effortlessly. Even the tails seemed to have changed, lengthened—two black wings cutting away at his thighs and ending at the backs of his knees.

Ryan raised his eyebrows in an "I told you so" way. He went into the bathroom and looked at himself in the mirror, smoothing out the lapels with his palms and running his fingertips along the sleeves.

"Fits like a *glove*!" He stepped into view, crossed his arms, and leaned against the doorway with a dopey grin on his face. "Don't I look damper?"

"*Damper?*"

"It's an old-fashioned word for 'handsome'."

"You mean 'dapper', dummy."

Ryan frowned and shifted back into the bathroom for another look. "Man, I look like Johnny Depp in this thing!"

"More like Benjamin Franklin," said Julie. "I'm taking it back to-morrow."

"No way. I'm keeping it."

"Seriously? You can't wear that thing out."

Ryan shut off the bathroom light and came back to the kitchen. Seeing him in it made her giggle.

"Why not?"

"Because people will think you're insane," she laughed.

"If those Goth dudes with the eyeliner and capes can get away with it, I think I can."

"If you start wearing eyeliner, we're done."

Ryan came towards her, put his hands on her hips, and then slid them around to her rear. A rotten smell wafted off the coat, causing her to stumble back, where she stepped directly onto the rest of the pizza. Ryan caught her as she slipped and fell, but Julie wriggled out of his embrace.

"*God,* that thing *stinks,*" she said.

"What?"

"That damn coat. Take it off. It needs to be washed." Julie un-spooled a handful of paper towels and began to wipe the sauce from her shoe.

Ryan sniffed at his shoulder and shrugged. "It smells fine to me."

"Maybe it's *you* then."

Ryan laughed. "Maybe."

"You should wear something under it. The lining's full of weird stains."

"You should see the inside of my regular jacket. It's like, tie-dyed with sweat."

"Lovely," she said, throwing the wad of sauce-stained paper towels into the trash.

Then Ryan's face changed, as if a brilliant idea had just occurred to him. "You know what I feel like? A smoke."

Julie looked up at him, mouth open. "You're kidding, right? Tell me you're kidding."

"Why not? It's my birthday. I found an old pack at the bottom of one of the boxes earlier." He went into the living room and came back with a half-smashed box of cigarettes. "Some got broken, but I think they're still good."

"Who *cares?* Remember why we quit in the first place? It was because you were coughing until you threw up. Remember that? Re-member not being able to take a deep breath without hacking? *I* do."

"Come on, Jule. We'll just have one."

"I don't think I want to revisit that. You do what you want, though."

She went into the bathroom and closed the door. She heard the window open, and when she came out she saw him outside on the fire escape, the cherry of his lit cigarette blazing like an evil eye. He had the coat collar raised, a jutting, black angle, like the bow of a ship. Julie mumbled a few expletives, pulled on her sweatshirt, and climbed out to join him. When he offered her one, she reluctantly took and lit it. The post-mortem pictures of smokers' chests from her textbooks flashed through her mind as the toxic cloud filled her lungs. After a few more puffs and coughs, she tossed it and watched it explode into a shower of magma-colored sparks on the pavement below. Ryan went on without a word, drawing the smoke in with the ease of a veteran inhaler and exhaling it into the night. As Julie watched him, she had a sudden, grim epiphany.

"You never really quit, did you?"

"Of course I did."

"Then why aren't you hacking your lungs out?"

He turned the lit end of the cigarette towards him and watched the thin, steady plume of smoke rising from it like steam. "I'm not sure ... they must have healed."

"And now you're ruining them again."

The wind blew, cold and sharp through the rickety bars of the fire escape, picking up dead leaves in the alley below and dragging them along the sidewalk. Julie shuddered and drew the zippered ends of her thin sweatshirt tightly around her. When Ryan took out another cigarette from the damaged pack and lit it with the previous one, Julie sighed and got up.

"I'm cold. I'm going in."

Back in the kitchen, she started unpacking boxes, wiping off plates and cups and arranging them in the cabinets. Then she moved on to cleaning up the remains of their makeshift dinner. Ryan came in as she was picking up the pizza box, the acrid stink of smoke trailing in after him. He took off the coat, draped it over a chair, and was about to say something when he started to cough.

At first the coughing was the normal throat-clearing type, but it quickly became worse. He started wheezing, choking, and his skin went grey, then a blotchy red; his eyes darkened and the cords of muscle in his neck stood out. Julie dropped the pizza box and caught him as he jackknifed over the chair and vomited on the floor. She steadied him, got him to the living room where, after a while, his breathing returned to normal and he was able to keep down some cold water. Julie helped him onto the futon, covered him with a quilt, then laid next to him, smoothing his dark brown hair while he shivered in his t-shirt and jeans under the blanket. His face was waxy and his irises were still a dull, murky color.

"I think we should go to the emergency room," said Julie.

"No, I'm fine now. You were right. I shouldn't have had that cigarette," said Ryan weakly. "When I saw them in the box earlier, I kept them to show you, to joke about how stupid it was. I never considered actually lighting one of the damned things. I don't know what I was thinking. And I made you do it, too. I'm sorry. I'm so sorry ..."

He broke off, teeth chattering too hard to continue. She stroked his face and kissed his clammy forehead.

"You're freezing. I'm going to turn up the heat."

Julie went to the thermostat and a few moments later the radiator began rattling. She cleaned the mess in the kitchen, turned off the lights, and went back into the living room. The apartment was hot now, but Ryan still shivered in his sleep. She stripped to her bra and underwear and lay down on top of the blankets beside him.

The streetlight cast long tree shadows across the living room ceiling. Julie lay there, watching the silhouettes of the huge boughs swaying as a storm gathered outside. Her eyes drifted into the kitchen, and to the coat. It hung on the back of the chair like a raven perched on a ledge. It seemed more to hover over the chair than rest on it, and Julie got the odd sensation that it was looking back at her. She turned on her side and slid under the edge of the blanket.

He never had a fit that severe, even at the pack-and-a-half-a-day height of it all. That lining's got bad stains ... could have been a reaction to it. Take it back tomorrow.

Her eyes narrowed, and then another voice, the one that spoke in cautionary tales, said:

Better do it before he gets up.

CHAPTER FOUR

She awoke to music. Not the buzzing cacophony of guitar and drums that Ryan was accustomed to blasting while showering or studying or (to her dismay) lovemaking. This was piano music, lovely and sweet. The delicate framework of notes drifted through the apartment like a pleasant scent. Julie rose and rubbed her lower back, stiff from another night on the thin futon mattress. She put her sweatshirt on and went into the kitchen. When she saw him, her heart sank.

Ryan was already wearing the coat; over last night's white t-shirt and a pair of bandage-colored boxer shorts. He sat at the table next to the little antennae radio, listening with his eyes closed and silently tapping his fingers on the table top in perfect time with each note.

"You look like a pirate stripper in that thing," said Julie.

Ryan opened his eyes and smiled. "*Arrrgh,* want me to take it *all* off?"

"Just that ugly coat." She bent down and kissed him. "Happy birthday."

"Thanks," said Ryan. He still looked weary from the previous night's ordeal, his face drawn, his eyes puffy and dim. "Want some coffee?"

"Sure." Julie poured herself some and joined him at the table.

"How are you feeling?"

"Fine, actually."

"I'm serious about that thing, you know. You shouldn't let it touch your bare skin. You could get a rash."

"I like how it feels. It's silky, like a second skin," he said. A series of low piano notes thundered out of the radio, distorting the little speaker. Julie gave it an annoyed look.

"What are we listening to?"

"Liszt's *'Les Funérailles'*."

"Since when do you like classical?"

"I've always liked solo instrumentals."

"*Guitar* solos."

He shushed her and closed his eyes again. Julie raised her eyebrows, picked up a magazine and looked through it while sipping the coffee. When the piece ended, Ryan opened his eyes and gave her a placid smile.

"So what do you want to do today?" she said, turning a page.

Ryan looked around the kitchen and sighed. "I suppose I should finish unpacking."

"I refuse to watch you toddle around the house, sorting through your crap in nothing but a weird coat and your underwear on your birthday. I'm taking you to dinner, and then I'm getting you a *proper* present."

"Speaking of presents, look what I found!"

Ryan plunged his hand into the coat's breast pocket and came out with a large ring. It was oval-shaped, with a glass-domed door encircled with tiny pearls that sat atop a tarnished gold band. Under the dome was a patchwork of plaited black hair interlaced with dark blue ribbon. He handed it to her.

"You found *this* in the pocket," said Julie, turning the ring in her fingers.

"Yup. Cool, isn't it?"

"*What* is it?"

"A ring."

"I can see that, smart ass. I mean what's with the hair?"

"I know. Weird, right? There's something engraved on the inside of the band, but all I can make out is the date."

Julie looked at the band. There was a date—1832—and a couple of stray letters obscured by a layer of dried, black crud. She scratched at it, but it wouldn't yield under a fingernail.

"Guess they forgot to check the pockets," said Ryan, grinning.

"That's impossible. If the coat's as old as this ring, that would make it a hundred and eighty. I'm sure *someone* thought to check the pockets in all those years."

"Yet, lo and behold ... a hidden treasure!" Ryan gestured at the ring with a flat, outstretched hand, palm upward. And then he laughed—a thin, shrill sound that Julie had never heard him make before. It raised the hair on her arms.

"I don't like it. It's creepy. And you're acting strange," she said, tossing it onto the table. The ring rolled across the surface and landed in Ryan's hand.

"Does this mean I'm not getting any more birthday kisses?" he said, frowning with mock disappointment.

"Not while you're holding that."

Ryan dropped the ring back into the pocket and held up his empty hands as if he'd just performed a magic trick. "How about now?"

Julie moved off her chair, came around the table, and kissed him once, then again, longer.

"At least that coat doesn't smell so funky today."

"It just needed a good airing out," said Ryan. He put his hand on her cheek. "It's an awesome gift, Jule."

She gave him an uncertain smile, then slid her hand up his leg and into his boxers. "I'm glad you like it."

"I like this more," he said.

CHAPTER FIVE

He insisted on wearing the coat to dinner.

She'd protested at first, but now, watching him walk down the crowded sidewalk, she thought the coat actually looked handsome on him, coupled with a white t-shirt and a pair of battered black jeans. Eccentric, to be sure, but not crazy. She liked the hesitation of the passers-by (men and women alike), that extra look they gave him as if they weren't sure whether or not he was a celebrity. And the coat itself didn't look as shabby now. The errant threads were gone and the tails didn't look so flat and matted.

"Did you wash that thing?" said Julie

"No. Why?"

"It looks ... healthier."

"Maybe it just needed to be re-broken in."

"A hundred-something-year-old coat?"

"It's probably been baking in some attic forever. It's bound to be a little stiff. Just need some new life."

"I suppose."

The sun had sunk behind the city, casting an orange halo behind the dark, monolithic skyscrapers in the distance. As they walked along the single-story row of shops comprising the neighborhood's shopping district, Ryan pulled a long-stemmed white clay pipe and a bag of loose leaf tobacco from the inside pocket of the coat. Julie stared in disbelief as he packed and lit it.

"Where the hell did *that* come from?"

"It was in the coat."

"You can't be serious."

"I am."

"Why are you smoking it?"

"Well, I've been thinking. I've got this terrible urge to smoke —"

"After what happened —"

"Before you freak out, let me explain. Obviously, after last night, I know I can't smoke cigarettes. But I realized—I *can* smoke a pipe!"

Julie crossed her arms over her chest. "How do you figure?"

"There's no inhaling with a pipe—it's all just puffing. Watch." The tobacco crackled and hissed as he drew a deep pull off the long stem and blew the smoke out in thick, wreath-like rings. Julie watched the grey shapes pulse, quiver, then dissipate against the sunburst sky.

"When did you learn to do that?"

"I don't know ... a long time ago."

"I don't remember seeing you do it before."

"Well, it's been a while."

"I hope you boiled that thing before you put your lips on it," she said, starting up the sidewalk ahead of him.

They reached the restaurant a short while later—a mid-priced Indian place that they ordered take out from at least twice a week. Ryan stowed the pipe inside the coat and went to open the door, but his hand hesitated on the handle. He grimaced up at the neon sign, then turned to Julie and said under his breath, "Do you really want to eat here?"

"Do *I*? It's *your* favorite restaurant."

"I know, I know ... it's just ... I think we could do a little better than *this*."

"What do you mean *better*?"

"Well, it seems silly to eat this foreign fare when we've got perfectly good American restaurants just a short stroll away."

"Stroll? What, are you in character now in your fancy new coat?"

Ryan frowned, took his hand off the door, and stepped back.

"Look, it doesn't matter to me," Julie said. "It's your birthday dinner. Wherever you want to go, we'll go, okay?"

"Thanks, Jule."

"So ... where then?"

Ryan thought for a moment. "Downtown."

CHAPTER SIX

They left the trendy neighborhood and took a bus to the old part of the city. Julie followed Ryan as he navigated the narrow brick streets, the coattails lashing out at her like black tongues. He cut down a winding, shadowy alley and stopped before a lantern-lit stone stoop. Above the crooked green door hung a sign from a cast-iron curl projecting from the side of the old building. The gilt letters read: **The Dancing Trout, Est. 1835**. Under the words was a pair of golden crossed fish, their mouths agape in death.

"This will do!" he cried.

Julie looked at the sign and scrunched up her face. "Looks expensive."

"I'll help pay."

"It's supposed to be *my* treat, remember?"

Ryan leaned forward and took her hand. "Come on, Jule. This could be one of those nights that we talk about years from now."

His face looked strangely different to her in the gas light, narrow and more angular, as if he hadn't eaten in a couple days. She'd always teased him about having a grapefruit for a head, but in this light his face had definition, a shelf of cheekbone and the outline of a chin. Julie supposed it was just a trick of the light, but he did look *thin*. She looked up at the golden dead fish and sighed.

"Let's hope I don't have to max out my credit card."

Ryan smiled and opened the door for her with a low, gentlemanly bow.

CHAPTER SEVEN

She'd expected something else that night—tandoori chicken and naan—Ryan plowing into his food without waiting for her own plate to arrive and talking with his mouthful. Instead he pulled the chair out for her, polished his cutlery, and discussed clarets with the sommelier. He ate poached herring (which he expertly removed from the bone) with horseradish cream and fresh dill, boiled potatoes with rosemary, new green peas, and a half-loaf of rye bread, all of which he ordered off the "Bill of Fare." After dinner, he had a post-meal sherry, sipping it with visible delight and wiping off the rim of the glass when he'd finished.

After dinner, they went down to the bar in the restaurant's basement, had a bottle of wine each, and were quite drunk on the walk home. Ryan smoked the clay pipe incessantly, and even Julie took a couple draws off it despite her promise to herself.

When they got back to Ryan's, Julie got naked and lay on the futon. Ryan undressed from the waist down and joined her.

"You can't make love in that thing."

"Why not?" said Ryan.

"Because the tails will get in the way," said Julie, slapping at them.

"All right, no tails." He slid his arms out of the coat and tossed it on the floor next to his pants. Immediately his expression became grave, as if he'd just been told some terrible news. His eyes darkened, his skin went death white, and his breath began to puff out in visible clouds. Suddenly, he collapsed to the floor, shivering so violently she was sure he was having a seizure.

Julie rushed to him, put her hands on him, and then drew them back in shock—his skin felt like refrigerated meat. After a few seconds of shock, she got hold of herself and dragged him onto the futon, where he whimpered and moaned, his head lolling deliriously on the pillow. Then, to her horror, he cast his head to one side and coughed a spray of red onto the white pillow case.

Julie's mind went into nurse mode: *Oh my God, it's TB ... How in the hell did he get TB?* She tried to cover him with the blankets but he was sprawled out across them, so she grabbed the first thing that was near—the coat—and covered him with it. She grabbed her purse, found her cell phone, and was dialing for an ambulance when he went still.

No, no no ...

Julie shook him, slapped him. "Ryan. *Ryan!*"

Ryan choked, gasped, and at last began breathing again. But Julie's relief quickly turned to unease as he rose, like a marionette brought up by ghostly hands, and settled with his back against the wall. He'd stopped shivering and his face was flush with color, yet something was different; his manner was altered, subtly. It was the way he sat there, unnervingly still, with the coat wrapped around him like a giant snake; the way he stared at her through those cloudy green eyes with a lewd smirk, his teeth stained a faint shade of rust. It spooked her. He raised the collar, folded his long fingers in his lap, and said:

"You're bare as the behind of a stagecoach horse, my love."

Julie looked down at herself, absently registering what he said, then crossed her arms over her bare breasts and began to cry.

"What the hell is going *on*, Ryan?"

He gave her a perplexed look. "What do you mean?"

"You were coughing up *blood!*" Julie said, smearing her tears. "It's that fucking pipe ... I *told* you ..."

"Blood?" said Ryan with mock horror. "Where?"

"All over the pillow!"

He looked down at it. "Ah."

"I have to take you to the hospital."

Ryan's grin faded. "No."

"I think you were having a seizure or something —"

"I'm not going to the hospital, Julie," he said. There was an ominous finality in his tone.

"You *have* to go! Something's wrong, Ryan, that coat —"

"*NO.*"

The sharpness of the word struck her like a blast of cold wind. Julie stared at him a moment, then got up and gathered her clothes.

"Fine. But I'm not going to be the one explaining to your parents when you end up in intensive care."

She went into the bathroom and slammed the door. When she came out, she saw the pipe bowl glowing on the fire escape. Anger brought on the tears this time. She considered going back to her dorm, but no buses ran that late and she felt too drunk to walk all that way.

Julie went back into the living room, where she stripped off the bloody pillow case and threw it in the trash. Then she crawled on the futon and pulled the blanket over her head. She lay there a long time with her disjointed thoughts, replaying what had happened in her mind and trying to make sense of it. After what felt like an hour, she heard him crawl back through the kitchen window. The musky stink of pipe smoke drifted into the room like a bad omen. Through slitted eyes, she watched him move through the kitchen and sit at the table. The radio clicked on and the somber notes of a cello began, lilting through the dark apartment like a dismal voice. She listened to him humming along, mirroring every note, and began to feel very frightened.

CHAPTER EIGHT

Julie woke in the silent apartment with a wine headache. Ryan wasn't in bed. She got up, went into the kitchen, and found a note on the table.

Jule,

I have to meet with Prof. Rickman after class, and then have some research to do at the library. See you later this evening? Perhaps you'll give me a chance to make good on last night's intimate debacle.

Love,

Ryan

Julie sat down and re-read the note, frowning at the florid, spidery handwriting, more akin to the signers of the Declaration of Independence than Ryan's usually illegible, D-average, sixth-grader scrawl. And then there was the content. He didn't have Rickman's class that day; he'd never set foot in the library once as long as she'd known him, and *intimate debacle?* There was no mention of the coughing attack, of the blood, of anything that had happened after he'd taken off the coat —

The coat!

Julie looked up, scanning the immediate vicinity. It wasn't in the kitchen. She searched the bedroom closet, the hooks behind the bathroom door. It wasn't in the living room either. But she did see something on the floor next to the futon. At first she thought it was a spider standing atop the carpet pile, but as she got closer, she saw it was the ring. A chill went through her. She was bending to pick it up when the noodly guitar ringtone of Ryan's phone started up. Julie jumped and spun around. The phone rang again. It was coming from his backpack, propped against a pile of boxes under the bay window. Julie unzipped the bag and looked inside. All his textbooks and notebooks were there. She checked the phone but didn't recognize the number.

Before leaving for class, she flipped over his note and wrote:

Ryan,

Not sure where you are or why you're lying, but if you decide to act normal later, give me a call.

Julie

Then she set the ring on top of the note and left.

CHAPTER NINE

Ryan did call, but not until much later that evening. He asked her to come over. He said he had a big surprise.

When Julie got to the house, she saw a stack of broken-down cardboard boxes beside the trash bins on the tree-lined lawn. *At least he got something done today,* she thought as she searched for her keys. The mournful wail of a viola filled the stairwell as she climbed to his apartment. When she opened the door, she dropped her purse in shock.

It was the same room she'd woken up in, but nothing about it was the same. Now it looked like a parlor from the Federal period instead of a college crash pad. Lush candlelight glowed from white tapers stuck in silver holders. An ornate wooden bookshelf stood against the far wall, its shelves lined with rows of identical, old, leather-bound volumes. The futon was gone, and in its place stood a settee with royal blue upholstery. The music came from the horn of a Victrola standing on a claw-footed side table beside the sofa. Early lithographs of the city, rendered in faded ink and pastel shades, hung above fauteuils on either side of the bay window.

The apartment was warm and redolent with something delicious. Julie went into the kitchen and found Ryan at the table with his back to her, sipping ruby-colored wine from a fine cut-crystal glass. He was wearing the coat. The broad shoulders rose above the back of the chair like black cliffs. The table was draped with a red cloth and set with silver serving dishes filled with food. Boiled lobster on green garnish ringed with sliced lemon, poached salmon resting on a lattice-work of braised asparagus stalks, a tureen of clam chowder dashed with freshly ground nutmeg, crusty bread on a flat serving tray ringed with pads of shell-shaped butter. Flatware gleamed golden in the candlelight from a candelabrum set at the center of the table. Linen napkins folded into fancy shapes stood on pewter chargers, and on the counter beyond were two bottles of fine French wine—one red, one white—the red uncorked.

Julie flipped on the kitchen light. Ryan turned around, shielding his eyes with his arm.

"Darling, if you please! That light is positively *dreadful*!"

"Sorry."

She turned it off, but in that instant she'd seen something inexplicable—streaks of grey in his dark hair. She went to him and ran her fingers through it. Ryan looked at her as if she'd gone mad.

"What did you do?"

"What are you talking about?"

"You dyed your hair!"

"No, I didn't."

"You're *grey*, Ryan!"

He shrugged. "It was bound to happen one day, I suppose."

"I'm not an idiot, you know."

"Of course you're not, my love."

She lifted the handle of the ladle stuck in the chowder and let it drop. "And this? Where did all this food and furniture come from?"

Ryan gave her a guilty look that Julie had seen before, and then she understood—the month's stipend had arrived.

"I don't think your parents would be too thrilled with all this. They send you money to *live* on, not to blow on whatever crazy shit you're into that week."

"And *live* we shall," said Ryan, uncorking the bottle of red. He snatched the glass beside her place setting and poured her some wine. "I know you prefer white, but that bottle will go better with the second course. I thought this young-bodied red would make a nice *vin avant le repas*."

Julie looked at him. "It's fine," she said.

He clinked her glass with his own, then sniffed, swirled, sipped, and savored the wine.

"Ah, now *that's* a fine claret." He set the glass on the table and smiled at her. "Are you hungry?"

"I am, actually. All I ate today was vending machine garbage."

Ryan looked aghast. He pulled out the chair for her and offered his hand. Julie went to take it, but withdrew when she saw the ring on his finger.

"Why are you wearing that? I told you I don't like it."

"It's just a ring, Julie."

"Take it off, Ryan. Please. I don't want to look at it. It's eerie."

Ryan huffed, took the ring off, threw it into the silverware drawer behind him, and slammed the drawer shut. The music stopped and he got up to change the record. While he was in the other room, Julie grabbed the ring out of the drawer and threw it out the kitchen window. She heard it hit the brick wall of the neighboring house, heard the glass dome crack before it fell into the shadows of the alley below. A string of minor-key piano notes preceded Ryan into the kitchen. Julie was back in her seat before he returned. He served them each some of the food, sat down, and shook out his napkin with a dramatic flourish.

"Where's the futon?"

"That ghastly thing? In the bedroom for now." Ryan surveyed the feast. "Shall we?"

"Why did you lie to me in your note this morning?"

Ryan folded his hands and looked at her evenly. "Because if I hadn't, all of this wouldn't have been a surprise," he said, gesturing at the table. "I didn't know you'd find me out." He held his fork up like a wand, an asparagus stalk impaled on it. He ate it, then pointed the tines at her. "Quite clever of you indeed."

"It was easy. You left your bag and phone."

"Good thing I did, too. Imagine if the blasted thing started ringing at the bookseller! The humiliation!"

Julie nodded slowly and took a bite of salmon. It was delicious. "So where did you go?"

"I took the ferry to the Point. You know, there are some *very* fine grocers there. An open-air market as well." He drained his glass, uncorked the red, and topped off her glass before refilling his own. "And who would have guessed that all this time we were but a boat's ride away from an exceptional cache of rare antiques? And the amount of —" He broke off, scratching at the sides of the coat and wincing. "Wool *does* give one a devil of an itch."

"Well, you've also been wearing the same thing for three days."

Ryan didn't comment. He picked up his lobster and cracked it, separating the tail from the body, and began removing the meat with a small picking fork. "There is one thing you'll be happy to learn. I've decided to retire the pipe."

"Thank God for that."

They ate without saying much more. After finishing most of the food and both bottles of wine, Julie looked at the wreckage of the meal and shook her head.

"I can't believe you made all this. Where'd you get the recipes?"

Ryan grabbed a book with a tattered binding off the counter and handed it to her. The worn cover read "American Cookery" in ornate, silvery capitals.

"It's the bible of East Coast cuisine," he said.

Julie opened it. On the flyleaf was the city's name and a date: 1833. She flipped through the yellow-tinged pages, admiring the fine-lined illustrations; shucked oysters arranged atop sea roughage in a woven basket, crab anatomies, detailed vegetable renderings.

"They're beautiful. So delicate ..."

Ryan stared at her with his cloudy eyes and passed his cool fingertips down her cheek. Julie shuddered, but not in a good way.

"So are you," he said.

CHAPTER TEN

She let him keep the coat on as he made love to her that night. She tried to get into it but couldn't. His body felt so heavy on hers, his skin so cold.

CHAPTER ELEVEN

In her nightmare, Julie awoke to a raspy moan coming from the living room closet. There was a frantic rapping on the door, terribly magnified, as if the sound was bouncing off the walls of a fishbowl. Suddenly, the door swung open; the handle smacked the wall—then silence.

Julie sat upright, staring through the gloom of the apartment. A strand of shadow emerged in the darkness, inching out of the closet like a tendril of vine seeking a column. It slithered along the doorframe, planted itself, and then unfurled into a little black hand. Then the rest of the shadow moved slowly into view. It was in the shape of a young girl, its skin, clothes, and tangled mass of hair all the color of burned toast. It came toward Julie on unsteady legs, plumes of smoke drifting from its open black maw as it cried,

Papa, help me, Papa, help me. Papa, please ...

It was on her now, the plea howling in Julie's ears, its ashy breathe surrounding her like a thick fog. The smell of burning was gagging.

Papa, help me, papa, helllp meeeee HELLLLP MEEEEEE!!

Julie backed up on the bed and fell into Ryan's arms. He wrapped his hands around her waist. She looked down and saw they were bones, and when she turned to him, what she saw wasn't Ryan's face, but a grinning skull with grey-black hair clinging to patches of rotted scalp. It pulled her into a tight embrace, her face smashed into the coat. The smell of rot filled her lungs. It lowered its bared teeth to her ear and whispered:

Sooo well made. And it keeps well ...

Julie woke with the feeling of the skeleton hands around her waist. She lay there, shaking, drawing deep breaths until the dream slowly receded, like a black curtain pulled back from a sunny window. Ryan lay asleep next to her with the coat collar raised. Gently, she lifted back the edge, looked, and was relieved to see skin and not bone.

The apartment was roasting. Julie took out her phone and checked the time. She was late. It was noon and her first class started at one. She got up quickly, turned down the heat, then walked into the living room to check the closet. The door was closed.

After getting ready, she poured some coffee into a to-go cup and dumped in some sugar. When she opened the drawer for a spoon, she shrieked.

The ring was there, hooked around the blade of a paring knife. The glass dome was shattered, the ugly patch of black hair now in plain sight. Julie looked out at the alley. In her mind, she heard the sound of it striking the brick wall. *Had he seen me throw it? Did he*

157

actually go out and get it? She touched the hair; it was still soft and pliable, as if freshly shorn. The ribbon, in contrast, was dry and brittle and stuck to the rim of the compartment with a rust-colored gunk. When she tried freeing it, it crumbled in her fingers. The feeling sent spider legs crawling up her neck.

"You saw her, too."

Julie spun around. Ryan was standing in the archway between the rooms with the coat buttoned to the top. It was now the color of ebony, boxy and stiff; the tails curving around him like a swallow's wings ready to take flight. But Ryan himself looked wilted within it, hands limp at his waist, his head hanging to one side as if his neck couldn't support the weight. His eyes were their normal color again, but sodden and red lined, as if he hadn't slept.

"Ryan!"

"So sad, isn't it? So very sad ..."

"What is it? What's wrong?"

He came toward her with his arms outstretched. At first Julie thought it was for a comforting embrace, but then she realized he wanted the ring. He took it and held it in his fingertips, stroking the hair and weeping.

"They couldn't find her ... they could hear her inside, but the fire was too hot. She thought she could hide ... she thought she could hide from it ..."

Julie put a hand on his face—it was like touching a marble effigy. The skin under the collar looked irritated. She folded it down, surprised at how hot it felt in contrast to his body—like an electric blanket set on high—and examined his neck. There were patches of maroon there, and that smell again—not body odor, but something more instinctually alarming. It was faint, but still it was there.

"*Dammit*, Ryan! I *told* you you'd get a rash from that thing!" She went to the bathroom and returned with a tube of ointment. He refused to take off the coat, so she had to apply it under the collar. Ryan grimaced but never took his eyes off the ring.

"You're staying home today. And you're taking a shower."

Ryan gave her a weak nod. She led him to the bathroom, flipped the toilet lid down, and planted him on it while she turned on the shower tap, testing it until the water was warmish so as not to further aggravate his skin. When it was the right temperature, she went to help him undress, but he clutched the coat closed at his chest and wouldn't let go.

"Ryan, please. I'm already late as it is."

"I can undress myself."

"Are you sure?"

Ryan gave her a condescending look.

"Alright. I'll be back around four-thirty. Call me if you need anything, okay? And keep putting that ointment on your neck."

Ryan nodded. She kissed his clammy forehead and hurried out the door.

CHAPTER TWELVE

The apartment was dim when she returned, and that bad smell—the *coat* smell, she thought—filled the room. A few fat, black flies drifted past her through the room. Her subconscious first picked up the sound, though being as common as it was, Julie didn't hear it right away. She crossed the living room and was opening the windows when it suddenly occurred to her—

The shower was still running.

She ran to the bathroom and turned on the light, her heart quickening when she saw Ryan slumped over on the toilet where she'd left him. He was staring at the floor with a thick line of drool hanging from his mouth, unbroken, stretching almost to his thigh. The ring had fallen from his hand and lay on the linoleum under the antique sink. Julie wiped his mouth and lifted his head, trying to rouse him. Finally, he blinked and looked up at her, his face full of shadows.

"What's wrong with me?" he whispered. A fly landed on his face and walked down the bridge of his nose. He didn't brush it off.

Julie lifted his head. His face felt like cold wax. "You need to lie down."

She took him by the shoulders, trying to lift him, but Ryan cried out as if her touch burned him. The rash on his neck looked worse, chaffed, as if it had been rubbed with heavy-grit sandpaper, and the further down it went, the darker it became. Julie unbuttoned the coat and gently lifted back the panels.

A smell like sun-spoiled meat hit her full on. She opened the coat wider and gasped. His arms and shoulders were covered in large, oval-shaped black and green sores oozing puss and blood. There were more infected areas beneath his t-shirt, ominous shadows like black mold covered up with white paint. Ryan winced as the inner lining peeled away from the slimy wounds.

"*Jesus*, Ryan … You have to go to the ER right now."

"Just give me some more of that skin stuff. That's all I need."

"This is way past that. You *have* to go to the hospital." Julie grabbed the coat to take it off, but Ryan wrenched it out of her hands and pulled it tightly around him. His cloudy eyes were filled with vitriol and Julie shrank back, afraid for a second that he was going to hit her.

"Just get the medicine," he said after a pause. "If it doesn't help, then we'll go to the hospital."

"Fine," Julie said. She got the tube of ointment out of the medicine cabinet, though only to placate him. She'd already decided to call for an ambulance once he was asleep. Then she saw the ring on the floor near the porcelain base of the sink and had an idea. She needed some answers, and if she couldn't bring the coat, the ring would have to serve in proxy. She picked it up and put it in her pocket, then very gingerly got Ryan to his feet and helped him to the bedroom.

"I'm going to run to the drug store for some peroxide and bandages. I'll be right back."

Ryan was lying on his back with his arms crossed over his chest and his eyes closed. She didn't like the look of it.

Be quick, the cautionary voice said.

CHAPTER THIRTEEN

There were other people in the vintage store this time—a few college students eyeing a red leather couch and a couple considering a chandelier. The clerk stood behind the counter in a Hawaiian shirt dotted with pepperoni stains. His eyes narrowed as she approached. Julie took out the ring and put it on the glass. He looked at her as if she'd set down a tarantula.

"I'm not interested in that."

"I'm not asking you to buy it."

"Then why'd you bring it?"

"I want to know what it is."

"It's a ring."

"It's more than that. And you know it."

"I don't deal in relics."

"What do you mean *relics*?"

"Human remains."

The man considering the chandelier looked up and scratched at his mustache.

"It's just hair."

"Hair cut off a dead person."

Julie gave him a bewildered look. The clerk glanced at the other people in the store and lowered his voice.

"It's called mourning jewelry. A hundred odd years ago it was common practice to cut the hair of the recently dead and use it in a brooch or ring or locket. Sometimes they made bracelets out of it. There's inlaid ribbon on this one which probably belonged to the deceased." He hovered over the ring, arms crossed, and scrunched up his face. "It's in bad shape. Where'd you find it?"

"In the pocket of that coat you sold me."

The clerk laughed. "That coat's at least a hundred and fifty years old and has probably had as many owners. Guess what the first thing each of those hundred and fifty guys checked?"

"But it *was* there."

"Whether it was or not, I already said *I'm not interested.*" He grabbed a ruler sticking out of a can of pens next to the register and used it to push the ring towards her.

"I'm not here to sell you this ring. I'm here because I need to know where that coat came from."

"How the hell would I know?"

"Well, it was in *your* store."

"Things like that don't exactly come with certificates of provenance, you know. They just show up one day in boxes with other old clothes."

"Look, my boyfriend's been wearing it for the last three days.

The lining's all stained and he's got this bad rash ..."

"That's not my problem."

"What do you mean it's *not your problem*? You sold me the damn thing and now —"

"No one told him to put it on."

"So you're not going to accept *any* responsibility then?"

The clerk pointed to an "All Items Sold As-Is, No Returns" sign and for the first time gave her a "have-a-nice-day" smile. Julie wanted to scream at him, to smack the grin off his face, but what she did was give an exasperated grunt before turning and walking out of the store.

"Hey, wait! I don't want this!" the clerk yelled after her. He looked down at the ring. After a moment of silent deliberation, he used the ruler to sweep it into the trash. Then he tied the bag, took it out back, and threw it in the dumpster. Meanwhile, the man with the mustache went out the front door and followed Julie down the sidewalk.

"Excuse me, Miss," he called after her.

Julie stopped and turned around as the man approached.

"What color are the stains?"

"What?"

"The stains on the jacket. Are they white or brown?"

"Brown," she said. "Why?"

The man looked at her for a long moment before speaking again. "Listen. I'm going to tell you something, but I want you to know beforehand that it's only a *theory*."

Julie nodded slowly and he continued.

"Grave robbing was very common around the time that coat was made. Students needed cadavers to dissect, and since the law then stated that only suicides and executed criminals could be used for that purpose, schools would hire resurrectionists to exhume bodies."

"So you think the coat came off a corpse? Why would they save it if they only wanted the body?"

"Usually the robbers would throw the clothes back in the empty coffin. But sometimes if they were in a hurry, they'd just deal with them later. Clothes were expensive then. I imagine a finely tailored coat—burial dress or not—would've been hard to just throw out in those days."

In her mind, Julie saw Ryan in the coat, lying on the bed with his hands crossed over his chest.

It's well made ... and it keeps well.

Julie managed to gasp out a "Thank you" before turning and sprinting down the street.

CHAPTER FOURTEEN

The house was black and still. The dark shapes of antique furniture crouched along the walls like hiding burglars. All the windows had been opened and the wind moaned through the screens, animating the long, sheer curtains.

Julie walked slowly toward the bedroom. Ryan wasn't there. There were large, brown stains on the bed where he'd lain. Flies bounced across the surface like kids on a playground. As she was watching this, she heard a distant *thump*. Her ears rose instinctively and the breath froze in her throat. She listened for it again, but all she heard was buzzing—on the bed sheets, on the wind, in the empty lobster shells in the kitchen trash can.

"Ryan?"

A second *thump*, from the living room, came in response. She crossed over the kitchen threshold and called to him again.

Silence. Then, a *click*.

The closet door opened and out stepped the man with the swamp weed-colored eyes, dressed in Ryan's shirt and shorts, and the coat. His face and hands glowed like moonlight and his black hair, streaked with silver, rose off his head like dark flames. He grinned that theater mask grin—drama and comedy blended into a terrifying leer—then let out a shrill laugh before turning and running down the apartment stairs.

Julie followed, chasing him down the street and screaming. The man was already a good distance ahead of her, bounding down the sidewalk with long-legged strides, laughing and mocking her pathetic cries. She ran as hard as she could but couldn't close the gap. He seemed to know this, seemed to be toying with her. Then something began to appear, hanging off the coattails—something white and textured, like a snake molting skin. The shape lengthened, became a form—a body with incorporeal legs trailing and arms gripping the tails as it whipped like a flag in a high wind. The form became more defined, and then suddenly Ryan's round face was looking back at her, his eyes full of terror and knowing, his mouth open in a silent scream. As the man rounded a corner, the white Ryan form detached.

Julie stopped, clutching a hand over her mouth as she watched him thin into an amorphous white mist. The mist hovered for a moment above the street, like a cloud of exhaust from a passing car. And then it was gone.

ABOUT THE AUTHORS

Richard Black lives in Cork City, Ireland, and grew up in the seaside town of Kilkee, County Clare. He is an aspiring author and filmmaker specializing in horror and dark urban fantasy.

Sebastian Bendix is a Los Angeles-based writer and musician, as well as host of a popular midnight horror film series, Friday Night Frights at the Cinefamily. He attended school at Emerson College for writing and has had pieces published in both in print (Mean Magazine, Sanitarium Magazine) and online (CHUD.com and Encounters Magazine). He has written several screenplays in the fantasy/horror genre, one of which, The Black Cradle, is in development as an independent feature. The Patchwork Girl was his first foray into the world of prose fiction. His second novel, The Stronghold, is nearing completion and will be out to publishers in 2015.

Joshua Rex writes scary stories in the Midwest, USA. His work has appeared in several anthologies, magazines, e-zines, and podcasts. He lives in an old house with his partner, the poet Mary Robles, and three gigantic cats.

And be sure to check out the latest Grave Marker release

(available for Kindle, Kobo, and Nook e-readers)

Tolerance
Hal Bodner

Children are disappearing from the streets of West Hollywood. The police are clueless, but Christopher Driscoll suspects he might know who is responsible. The trail leads to local new hot spot that has become THE place to eat. Has the owner been serving up finger-licking good baby barbecue, or has there been a HUGE mis-understanding?

www.ingramcontent.com/pod-product-compliance
Lightning Source LLC
Chambersburg PA
CBHW061214170626
46809CB00003B/1358